PARK RANGER

London life and a university course hold no appeal for Paul Graham, a happy-go-lucky teenager who wishes to try his hand at country life. When he is offered the job of Assistant Park Warden at Bearsdale National Park, he heads northwards without another thought.

But his new life is not an easy one. The Park Ranger, David Martin, had wanted an experienced man and the people of Bearsdale do not take easily to strangers.

Flung headfirst into a series of tough, thrilling adventures, Paul soon learns that life in the country is not as peaceful as it seems . . .

PARK RANGER

A CAROUSEL BOOK 0 552 52097 7

First publication in Great Britain

PRINTING HISTORY
Carousel edition published 1979

Carousel Books are published by Transworld Publishers Ltd.
Century House, 61-63 Uxbridge Road, Ealing,
London, W5 5SA:

Made and printed in Great Britain by the Guernsey Press Co., Ltd.,
Guernsey, Channel Islands.

PARK RANGER

by Chris McMaster

Illustrated by Trevor Parkin

CAROUSEL BOOKS
A DIVISION OF TRANSWORLD PUBLISHERS LTD

CONTENTS

PARK RANGER

by Chris McMaster

CHAPTER ONE

RABID

It was a fine day, late in July. David Martin, Senior Warden of Bearsdale National Park, stopped his battered landrover and got out to gaze at the wide landscape of moor and cloud-shadowed mountain which lay before him. David looked younger than his forty-four years. His face was deeply tanned by sun and wind, and his eyes had the keen weather-wise look of farmers and sailors. An old briar pipe stuck from his mouth, and the sharp mountain air blew a plume of tobacco smoke about him as he stood braced against the brisk westerly wind. David had spent many years as a ship's engineer, tinkering with the works of tramp steamers from Clyde to Cape Town. Later he had served with the Kenya Police, and then spent several frustrating months when that fell through behind a desk in London. Now he was where he wanted to be and would not have changed places with anyone in the world.

David's mind wandered back to the old days, before he came to Bearsdale three years ago, before he was born, in fact before the first motor vehicles penetrated this mountain wilderness. Once, David reflected, no man rode out here unarmed. This was Border country, where the King's writ did not run, and the ballads sung of cattle raiding and clan warfare. Here every man went armed against his neighbour and against the Scots. It was not so different now, he reflected wryly, except that the enemies he had to fight were pollution and fire, damage to the wildlife and the countryside, or strife between townsman and countryman.

David's thoughts were broken abruptly by the thunder of hooves. A strikingly lovely girl of about sixteen was riding a great chestnut stallion at full gallop towards him.

"Hello, Katie!" yelled David. "One of these days you'll go right into me!"

"Nonsense!" laughed Katie. "Nero knows when to stop — and I do too." Nero was breathing hard after their furious gallop and Katie calmed him with a friendly pat on the neck. "I hear you've got a new chap joining you."

"Right," said David, "Paul Graham, just out of school. I would rather have had an older man, someone who's done a bit, seen a bit of the world. Still, I expect he'll learn."

"I'm sure he will with you teaching him," said Katie. She set heels to Nero and was off like the wind. David watched her go, then put the clutch in and set off for home.

An hour later, Katie turned in at Scarsdale Farm, dismounted and made Nero comfortable for the night. Scarsdale had been her home for as long as she could remember. The big farmhouse of whitewashed stone, the yard with stables and barns, the wide view across the Moors towards Eskdale — she knew every stone of it, and loved it more than she even knew. Katie could dimly remember living in a tall house in London, when her father was still alive, but when her father had been killed in an air crash, her mother had started life afresh here in the mountains, practising her profession as a country vet now, and taking in one or two visitors in the summer.

Margaret Jackson was a sensible, attractive young woman, and the Dalesmen had grown to trust and like her. She had sat up all night to deliver a colt, gone through snowstorms to cope with a flock of ailing sheep, and dealt with sick cows and injured sheepdogs without fuss, and without asking more than the most modest fees.

Her daughter, Katie, was still at school much to her own disgust. Every morning, Margaret dropped her in Eskdale, six kilometres away, before doing her morning rounds — and every evening she picked her up again. This was the best time of the day when Katie could exercise her beloved Nero and the two mares, Bonny and Lady, that were kept for visitors. Katie was not stupid, but she did only fairly well at Eskdale Comprehensive. Her mind was forever on when she would leave school and be able to spend her whole time on the Farm, with the horses she loved. Still, today had been the last day of term and now the summer holidays stretched pleasantly before her. She would have endless time to dream. One day she might build up a training stable, ride in the point to point at Thorburn, perhaps even take part in the Badminton Cross Country . . . her thoughts were sent flying by Margaret banging a coffee pot down on the table.

"Katie," she said brightly. "Wake up! Coffee's here!"

Katie came to with a bump. "Sorry, Mum," she said. "I was miles away."

"You certainly were," remarked Margaret. "Any news in Eskdale?"

Katie sipped her coffee carefully. "Not that I know of," she replied. "Oh, there's a new lad joining David, I hear."

"So I hear," said Margaret, somewhat absent-mindedly. Katie stretched out her legs and gazed at her boots.

"About time somebody new turned up in Bearsdale, isn't it? Nothing new ever happens here."

****

As it was, Katie could not have been more wrong. For twelve hundred kilometres away, in France, events were taking place which would plunge David, Margaret and Katie too, into the grimmest adventure they had yet known.

Charlie Stubbs was standing in the lorry park at Cherbourg, swigging from a large bottle of red wine, and wolfing a loaf of French bread into which was stuffed a quantity of sliced Normandy ham. Charlie was a huge good-natured man, with a thatch of fair hair and a rough tanned face, who had been hauling long distance lorries across Europe for more than six years. Now as he waited for the Cross Channel Ship, he was snatching a few moments relaxation.

Lorries stood all about him, marked *'Marseille — Lyon — Dunquerque'* or *'Basel — Frankfurt — Antwerp'* or even *'Roma — Milano — Torino — Parigi'*. The air was filled with diesel fumes, and tough young men in worn berets and leather jackets — French, German, Italian and English, leaned against their vehicles, eating and drinking and smoking, while a loud speaker blared out pop tunes.

As Charlie munched, a battered looking dog approached. He could have been a retriever but there were a number of other breeds mixed in. One ear was torn and his coat was in shocking condition, but he grinned cheerfully at Charlie, and squatted in the dust, his ragged tail wagging hopefully. Charlie was an exceedingly sentimental man. At home in Wimbledon he kept an elderly cat and budgie to whom his wife and two boys were very devoted. But they had once owned a Cairn Terrier from a tiny pup until she died of sheer old age, and Charlie, though extremely fond of dogs, had never had the heart to replace her. This pooch reminded him of his Tartan somehow.

"Hello, Fella!" he exclaimed. "Want a bite then?" He tossed the dog a scrap, and the dog wolfed it instantly and looked up for seconds. "Is he yours?" asked Charlie of a passerby. Then seeing that he was a foreigner, continued in atrocious French, "Le chien, est il le votre?"

"Non Monsier," said the Frenchman, moving on, flicking his Gaulois in disgust. "The dog, he's nobody's. He belongs — how you say — to no one."

"Ah, what a shame!" said Charlie sadly. He chucked the dog the last of his roll, took another swig of wine and moved off towards his lorry. As he climbed into the cab he saw that the dog had followed him, and was sitting expectantly right in front of his front tyre.

"You can't come with me, wack," said Charlie. "I'm off to England!" The dog did not budge, but went on looking pathetically at him. Charlie sighed deeply. "I'm telling you, if you come with me you're going to be locked up for six months! Quarantine! The jug — compronez? You don't want that do you? Go away! Shoo!" Still the dog sat there grinning, both ears cocked. It was too much for Charlie. "Oh all right then!" he said. "Come on!" The dog leapt into the cab beside him, Charlie revved up the engine and they drove towards the waiting ship.

It was a clear summer's morning when the ship docked in Southampton, and Charlie drove his lorry to the Customs Post. A Customs Officer hurried over to check his papers and looked briefly around Charlie's cab.

"Had a good trip?" he asked. He knew Charlie well, for Charlie had been through these dock gates at least forty times in the past six years.

"Not bad," said Charlie cheerfully. "Strasbourg, Paris, Cherbourg. Now I'm off to Scoresby of all places!"

"Good luck," said the Customs Officer, waving him on. He had not looked into the back of the lorry, and so he did not know that there, hidden among the crates, lay the dog fast asleep. Charlie drove carefully out of the docks and through the bustling streets of Southampton for the road north.

That same morning, Katie was out exercising Nero up on the moors above Rodale Woods. The chestnut was fresh and high-spirited, and Katie had to use all her skill to keep him under control as they thundered across the grass. At last, flushed with exertion, she pulled him in. Nero had settled into a brisk trot when a burly man appeared over the brow of the hill with two sheep dogs and a large flock of sheep. Running ahead was a small bespectacled boy with an overgrown sheepdog pup frisking at his heels.

"Hello Jamie!" called Katie. "How's Rex?"

"He's fine," said Jamie proudly, beaming up at her. "In a few weeks I'm going to start training him."

Jamie's father, Alf Dutton, had by now caught up with them. "Training, he says!" he exclaimed. "There won't be any training, that pup. He'll have to stay a pet all his life, you mark my words! Here,

Bounce! Here, Gellert!'' He whistled an order to his sheepdogs and tramped on up the hill after his charges. Katie smiled after them and then set heels to Nero, speeding on down into the valley below.

A while later she turned in at Grimsdyke, past the sign of the Bear which bore the legend *'Bearsdale National Park, David Martin — Senior Warden.'* David's house had once been a forge, and it was still known to the local people as 'the Smithy'. Nestling into the barren hillside, the forge had withstood the winter storms of nearly two centuries, and from its lofty position commanded a magnificent view across the mountains to the west. Inside it was easy to tell that David was a bachelor. The enormous open fireplace had not been cleared out for weeks. The walls has disappeared under a motley collage of maps and posters, the oak table under papers and a pile of freshly washed socks. Well-thumbed books on rickety home-made shelves, mostly about mountaineering and sailing. In the corner a pot of coffee steamed on the hob and beside it David, pipe in mouth as usual, was battering away at his typewriter on a report on tourism.

"Hi," said Katie, peering over his shoulder. "Knee deep are you?"

"I always am," replied David, typing away determinedly. "The latest thing is the hill farmers, complaining about tourists. I mean what are we to do? People want to get out of the cities and into the national parks once in a while. They want to go hiking and pony trekking, and they want to drag their kids along with them. I'm not supposed to stop them."

Katie flopped down onto the bench by the fireplace. "Where is he then?" she enquired.

"Who?"

She sighed, "The new boy, of course, your deputy."

"He isn't my deputy, he's a trainee," muttered David, pulling one page out of his typewriter, and laboriously inserting a fresh one.

"You don't sound too happy about it."

"I'm not," said David. He tapped his finger on the map above him. "I mean, just look at this place. Nine hundred square kilometres of mountains, forests, nearly thirty kilometres of coastline. Bearsdale may not be the biggest national park in the country — but it's still a big area. I need help to look after that lot — trained help — haven't got time to play nurse-maid!"

During this tirade, Katie had picked up a poster from a pile stacked against the end of the bench. It was printed on a bright scarlet background, and showed the terrifying mask of a rabid dog with teeth bared. "What's this?" she asked, holding it away from her with two fingers.

"Just another poster they want me to put round," replied David, returning to his typing.

"Frightening, isn't it?"

David turned to give his full attention. "It's meant to be," he said quietly. "People just don't know what a risk they take if they smuggle dogs into this country. Rabies is a terrible thing."

Charlie was driving northwards at that very moment, whistling merrily. As soon as he had cleared Southampton, he had shifted the dog into the driving compartment, and now the battered mutt sat beside him watching the mountain landscape rush by and sticking his nose out of the open window from time to time to enjoy the breeze.

"What shall we call you then?" asked Charlie. "Spot? Rover? Doesn't seem right somehow, Rover, for a French dog. Pierre! That's it! That's what we'll

14

call you — Pierre!''

****

Paul Graham drove his beach buggy at top speed into Bearsdale. A stocky, freckled lad, only just past eighteen, he liked to take life as it came, and he was looking forward to being a Park Warden. His parents had died in a car crash when he was barely six years old, and his Uncle John had adopted him. For twelve years he had lived in a pleasant rambling house in Hampstead when he was not away at Boarding School. Uncle John ran a highly successful publishing firm, and his Aunt Carol was a top freelance photographer, so life at Hampstead was very comfortable. Indeed, Paul had had to fight quite a battle with his Aunt and Uncle to get them to agree to him giving up a university place and a future in his Uncle's business to become a Park Warden, with what seemed to them uncertain prospects and very poor pay. But Paul was used to getting his own way and now, as he bowled along in his garish purple beach buggy with his transistor blaring away and the stinging mountain air rushing round him, he had not a care in the world.

Suddenly he became aware of a girl riding a big chestnut stallion at full gallop along the track next to him. Paul was a strong swimmer, an expert skin diver, could manage a sailing boat with ease and climb mountains, but he had never had anything to do with horses. The girl was waving gaily to him as the buggy and the chestnut paced one another. Paul waved back. "Stay with him, cowgirl!" he yelled, and in sheer high spirits sounded his horn. Nero — for it was he — was taken by surprise. He shied violently, hit a ditch and went down. Katie rolled away out of the saddle and Paul, horrified, brought the buggy to a screeching halt and rushed over to Katie who was sitting in the heather feeling her ankle.

"Are you all right?" he called anxiously as he came up.

"No thanks to you if I am!" cried Katie furiously. "Don't you know better than to sound your horn near a horse?"

"I'm sorry!" he said, penitently. He offered to help her up but was shrugged away.

"I should think you are!" shouted Katie, climbing to her feet. Nero had stopped and was placidly cropping the grass a few feet away. The girl hobbled towards him.

"Can I help?" asked Paul uselessly.

"Oh, just get lost!" She caught at Nero's bridle and mounted him, cantering off without another word. Paul, red-faced, drove away in his beach buggy — this time less exuberantly.

Margaret had just finished afternoon surgery when a sour Katie got back. "Had a fall?" she enquired as Katie limped in.

"No, I was thrown!" exploded Katie. "That stupid boy!"

"What stupid boy?"

"That stupid boy in that stupid car! He shot up right under Nero's nose. Never heard of the Country Code. Townies. Why can't they stay in towns where they belong?" She started to trudge upstairs when the phone rang.

"Jacksons," said Margaret, putting down her mug of tea to pick up her notepad. "Hello, Alf," her expression changed, "Rex! Well, when did it happen? I see. Well keep him quiet, and I'll come round at once."

Katie had stopped on the stairs watching her mother's face. "What's up?"

"Young Jamie Dutton's pup, Rex. He's been hurt — hit and run car."

Soon afterwards, Margaret arrived at Alf's hill farm. There was a tractor in the yard and Alf was tinkering under the bonnet, but as Margaret turned in he left it and strode over to her, toying worriedly with his oily spanner.

"Hurt real bad, he is," he said. "Boy's out playing — I daren't tell him." He led Margaret into the little whitewashed kitchen where his wife, Alice, was cradling Rex on her lap. Margaret lifted the young puppy onto the table and examined him carefully. Blood matted his coat and there was no movement in his legs. He tried feebly to lick

17

Margaret's hand as she felt his bones, then uttered a low moan as her fingers ran along his back.

At last Margaret looked up. "I'm sorry Alf. There's nothing I can do. His back's broken — and he has internal injuries."

Alf and Alice stared back at Margaret in disbelief. "But he's Jamie's dog," whispered Alice. "There must be something...." Her voice tailed off.

"I'm sorry, there's nothing I can do for him. It would be cruel to keep him alive in this state. I doubt if he'd last a week."

"But.."

"I'll take him home with me," said Margaret decisively, "and do what has to be done. Rex won't feel anything — just go to sleep. Do you want me to tell Jamie that?"

"No," said Alf slowly. "Reckon that's a Dad's job. Thanks Mrs Jackson — I'll tell Jamie when he gets in."

****

Standing in the Warden's office, David was taking a long time to light his pipe, while Paul sat before him by the oak table, the duffle bag that held all his wordly belongings lying beside him. At the moment he was distinctly nervous, for David was quite clearly sizing him up.

"You were born in London."

"That's right."

"Lived all your life there?"

"Except for term time, yes."

"What makes you want to be a Park Warden?"

"I fancy the life, I always have."

At this, David gave Paul a questioning glance and then went back to his pipe.

"Do you know anything about it?"

"I've read some books — and I talked to a chap who served in Scotland....." He trailed off weakly and lowered his eyes under David's piercing gaze.

"I see," he said. He had managed to light his pipe and now slowly exhaled a puff of smoke. "You can drive of course."

"Yes, and I can climb." Paul said eagerly, feeling more positive.

"How do your parents feel about you living away?"

"My parents were killed in a car crash ten years ago. I've lived with my Aunt and Uncle ever since." Paul felt that this gruelling interview was never going to let up. However, David was not really a harsh man. His years abroad had taught him to size up problems and people carefully and then, and not until then, take judgement or action. Now he saw Paul sitting there, looking even younger than his eighteen years with his tousled hair and his faded denims and oversize jersey, and his heart warmed to him.

"I see," he said at last. "Well, I've fixed for you to stay here if you like — that's if you don't mind things being a bit rough and ready." Paul shook his head emphatically. "Anyway, why not stay here a few days while you get your bearings. If you find something better — well and good. But if you do decide to stay here — it's amazing what a bit of whitewash will do!"

David grinned in friendly fashion at Paul, and Paul could not help but grin back at him.

Meanwhile, at the Dutton's hill farm, things were far from pleasant.

"I want my dog back! I want my dog back!" Jamie's small face was blotched with tears. He took

19

his spectacles off and tried to wipe them, but he was crying too much to make a good job of it.

"Jamie," said Alf, helplessly. "There was nothing I could do about it. He was that hurt . . ."

"They could have cured him!"

Alice knelt down and took Jamie in her arms. "Jamie! Your father's told you — he was hurt very bad. Everyone's got to die sometime — even dogs. Rex had a good life..."

"I want him back!"

"Look son," said Alf, kneeling also. "I'll get you another dog. There's lots of bitches round here, you know. First litter...."

"I don't want another dog — I want Rex!"

Alf stood up brusquely. "We got to accept things sometimes," he said. "Come on, son. I've got to shift those ewes to the top of the pasture before nightfall, and I need a hand."

Alf strode out into the gathering dusk, whistling to Bounce and Gellert, and set out for the pastures with Jamie trailing behind. Alice watched them go from the kitchen door. Jamie did not bound along in front of his father as he usually did, but stumped into the distance, hands thrust into his anorak pockets, his specs misted with tears. There were tears too on Alice's cheeks as she watched them trudge up the hill. She wiped them away hastily and turned back to her cooking.

Alf strode across the moors above Thorburn with Bounce and Gellert running ahead and Jamie trudging along in the rear. As they reached the road, a large lorry hoved into sight and a hefty young man jumped out of the cab and ran over to them. "Scuse me!" called Charlie. "Can you put me on the road to Scoresby?"

"You're out of your way, mate," replied Alf.

"Go on about a kilometre, turn left, go on to the next cross roads, turn left again and it's about eight kilometres on from there."

As he spoke, Pierre leapt from the cab behind him with his tail wagging and lolloped into Jamie's arms.

"He your dog, Mister?" Jamie asked.

"Yeah, sort of, I picked him up in France yesterday."

"Oh, he's lovely!" Jamie cuddled Pierre who, unused to all this affection, responded with an ecstacy of tail thumping and face licking.

The two men grinned at the sight of this, and Alf said in a confidential manner, "He lost his own dog today in an accident."

"Did he now?" said Charlie sentimentally, thinking back on his own Tartan. "Would you like to have him then?"

"You can't do that!" exclaimed Alf.

"Why not? Come to think of it, I've no place for him. Give me a fiver for him if you like and we'll call it quits."

Alf hesitated, but Jamie burst in, "Can I have him? Please, Dad!"

"All right," said Alf reluctantly. "If you really want him," then turning to Charlie, "Are you sure a fiver's enough?"

"Well, call it a tenner," said Charlie equably. "His name's Pierre, by the way. I called him a French name see, 'cos of his homeland."

"What about quarantine?" asked Alf, giving the mongrel a doubtful look as he eased two crumpled five pound notes from his wallet.

"What's that?" said Charlie. He pocketed the tenner and hopped back into his cab. Within moments the lorry was out of sight.

"Come on Pierre! Come on boy!" cried Jamie, running ahead as before. Pierre followed wagging his tail, and Alf went after them, smiling to himself. He thought his tenner well spent.

Back at the farm, Alice was less enthusiastic. She wrinkled her nose at Pierre, "Needs a bath, doesn't he?"

"I'll give him one," Jamie put in.

"Where did you find it?" she enquired, turning to her husband.

"Chap we met on the road gave it to him. Chap in a lorry that is, I gave him a tenner for it.."

"A tenner!" exploded Alice. "What are you up to, throwing away good money like that....."

Alf cut in strongly. "Look Alice, the boy's broken hearted — at least he was. Now he's got a new dog, and no harm done to anyone. Worth a tenner isn't it?"

"What about quarantine?" asked Alice.

"He didn't bother," Alf replied, looking and feeling a little sheepish.

"Well, I really don't know!" Alice looked still more doubtful.

"Please, mum!" pleaded Jamie. "I'll look after him, really I will." So it was settled, and before long Pierre was reluctantly having the first bath of his life. Then, after a more welcome supper of scraps, he fell asleep on Jamie's bed. Alf removed him to the barn. He didn't hold with dogs living in the house he told Jamie firmly. What was good enough for Bounce and Gellert was certainly good enough for Pierre.

Over at Grimsdyke, the other newcomer to the district was tucking into a hasty dinner of bacon and eggs.

"All right?" asked David, with his mouth full. "I'm afraid I'm not much of a cook."

"Fine," said Paul, wiping the last of the egg yolk from his plate with a hunk of bread. He was ravenous after the long drive from London. "I would like to help with the cooking if I may, I learned to cook a bit last year when I went sailing."

"Great," said David. There were a few minutes silence as they cleaned up the remains of their meal, then he remarked, "By the way, when we've tidied things up, I thought we'd go over to Margaret Jackson's. She's our local vet. Lost her husband ten years ago. Lives with her daughter Katie. You'll like them, I think."

When they arrived, Margaret was in the act of rushing out on an urgent case. Susie, the local girl who acted as their housekeeper-cum-receptionist, was trying to clear the table while Katie dozed over her tea.

"I'll be back about ten, I hope," said Margaret, picking up her veterinary bag. "If Colonel Ransom calls, tell him I'll drop over tomorrow — Oh, and I'm expecting a call about Justice, at Kirby's place, it may be a difficult birth — it was last time."

"Right-oh, Mrs Jackson," said Susie cheerfully, whisking the tablecloth from under Katie's nose. She was a plump, ruddy, country lass with a jolly, easy-going nature, and Margaret would have felt lost without her.

David and Paul caught Margaret just as she was getting into her Rangerover.

"You shooting off!" exclaimed David. "I wanted you to meet Paul Graham, my new trainee."

"Hello," said Margaret warmly, shaking hands with him. "Sorry I can't stay — I've been rushed off my feet today. Oh, this is my daughter, Katie."

Katie had come out to investigate the sound of a new voice, but stopped at the sight of Paul. She gave him an icy look. "Yes, we've met."

****

Another blazing hot day dawned. Alice was bustling about in her kitchen, getting Alf off to work and Jamie to the village school.

"Come on, Jamie!" she scolded. "It's ten past eight. You don't want to be late on the last day of term!" Jamie nodded and munched faster on his cornflakes.

"How's your bike working?" asked Alf, as he filled a plate with scraps.

"Alright," mumbled Jamie, rather inaudibly, his mouth full of cereal. "Brake's a bit stiff, that's all."

Alf went across the yard and into the barn with the plate of scraps. "Pierre!" he called. "Here, boy!" A strange growling noise caused him to swing round, Pierre was crouching in the corner of the barn, glaring at him. As Alf approached he uttered another menacing growl. There was a fearsome glow in his eyes that was quite unnatural.

Alf backed hurriedly out of the barn, plate in hand, without a word. Back in the kitchen, Alice was still trying to get her son organised. Now he had mislaid his satchel and had been sent packing upstairs to find it. It was at that moment Alf returned to the kitchen. "Alice!" His tone was so serious that Alice stopped clearing the table and looked up in alarm. "The dog's sick — Pierre, I mean. Won't touch his food, just crouched there glaring at me."

"Better call Mrs. Jackson. Maybe he is sick — they don't have quarantine for nothing you know."

Jamie had found his satchel under his bed. Now

24

he paused on the stairs listening intently.

"Look if he is sick," he heard his father say. "They'll have to do something about it."

"You mean, Jamie would have to wait for him, until he's out of quarantine?"

"No, I don't mean that, Alice," came his father's grave voice again. "I mean if he's really sick they might have to put him to sleep."

Alf picked up the phone and dialled Margaret's number, sick at heart.

"What exactly is wrong with him?" asked Margaret when he was through to her. "I see! Yes, it does sound as if I should have a look at him. I'll call round as soon as I can."

Alf was hovering at the gate when she arrived. "I don't like the look of him, honest," he said, as soon as she had got out of her Rangerover, veterinary bag in hand.

"You were quite right to call me," Margaret said, as they entered the barn together.

"Well, I had to," said Alf, anxiously. "I mean, he was acting so strange..." Alf stopped abruptly. Pierre was gone. At that moment too, Alice rushed in, her face flushed with anxiety and panting for breath.

"Alf!" she cried. "Jamie's run off with the dog!"

"How do you know?" asked Margaret.

"I thought he'd gone off to school," Alice gasped. Her big hands fumbled and twisted at her apron skirt. "Then... then, I found his bike still here, and this note like."

Alf took it from her, read it and handed it to Margaret without a word. It was rather badly spelt but its meaning was clear enough.

'Dere Dad and Mum,' it ran, 'I herd what you sed about Pierre, and I'm taking him away were you *can't find him, ever.'* signed Jamie Dutton, with a P.S. *'I've taken sum bred, so you needn't worry about me — I won't be hungry.'*

Margaret turned to face Alf and Alice, her face tense and white. "How exactly was the dog behaving?" she asked quietly.

"Well, he was strange like," said Alf. "Didn't seem to know me — crouched down, growling, with his eyes glowing, if you know what I mean."

A horrible suspicion crept into Margaret's head. "Alf where did this dog come from?"

"He was a stray."

"Where did it come from?" she repeated. Alf and Alice exchanged glances.

"France," said Alice, somewhat timidly. She had a feeling what Margaret's reaction would be, and sure enough the explosion erupted.

"You brought a dog in from France. Without having it quarantined and vaccinated!"

"It wasn't me," said Alf, defensively. "It was this chap, this lorry driver. He said he'd picked him up in France. He must have smuggled it through."

Margaret took a deep breath to control her mounting anger. "Alf, that dog may have contracted rabies."

Stunned with horror, Alf tried to speak but could say nothing. At last came a whispered, "Rabies, we didn't think."

"You didn't think," choked Margaret, almost bereft of words. "Do you realise that rabies is sweeping across the continent like a forest fire! The only things keeping this country safe are the Channel and the quarantine laws! Do you know what happens to a human being if he's bitten by a rabid dog!"

Alice knew; she burst into an uncontrollable flood of tears.

David answered the phone. "Right!" he said briskly. "I'll contact Air Rescue — and the Police. Paul, you'd better take off in that beach buggy of yours. I haven't a vehicle to spare at the moment. Take this walkie-talkie, cover this area, west of Scarsdale —" he made a sweep across the map with his hand. "Keep in touch with me — and tell Katie to have a look too if you see her." Paul nodded and was gone. Then David switched on the RT link with Air Rescue.

"Colin!" he called. "Look, Colin. We've got a spot of trouble."

Air Rescue was simply a Nissen hut set high in the crags above Eskdale. The pilot was playing chequers with Nigel, his Number Two, when David's call came through.

"Yes, I've got that," said Colin, scribbling on the pad before him. "Small boy and dog — retriever type — north of Riddsdale. Right, I'm on my way. Out."

Struggling into their flying jackets, Colin and Nigel dashed to their helicopter. Minutes later, the vanes began to turn, swifter and swifter until the helicopter lifted slowly from the landing pad and flew north towards Riddsdale.

The hunt was on. Margaret was combing the mountain pastures in her Rangerover. David had driven in a more westerly direction. Twice he stopped, leapt out of his landrover and swept the desolate horizon through his binoculars, but there was no sign of his quarry. Desperately, he leapt back into his landrover and raced onwards. Once contracted, rabies acts with dreadful speed. David was fighting the clock and he knew it.

By now, Jamie and Pierre were high up among the peaks of Riddsdale. The tiny boy paused for breath amid the tumbled rocks. He took off his spectacles and wiped them, then put them on again and rose to his feet. "Come on Pierre!" he called. Pierre hesitated, belly down in the powdery gravel, growling faintly, but Jamie did not hear him. Instead, in the distance, he could hear an ominous whirring sound, growing louder until it was quite unmistakable. Suddenly he saw the helicopter flying low in his direction.

"Come on!" he screamed. "They mustn't find us!" He seized Pierre by the scruff of the neck and dragged him under the shelter of an overhanging rock as Colin flew over. The helicopter came so close that the blast from its spinning blades ruffled Jamie's fair hair and Pierre's tousled coat. The noise was deafening. Seconds passed slowly, and then the helicopter flew on. Jamie waited until it was safely out of sight before moving on, ever upwards, with Pierre.

Down on the valley floor, Paul stopped his beach buggy by an outcrop of rocks, pulled out his binoculars, and swept them steadily across the mountain slopes. No sign of life, except for a flock of sheep grazing peacefully in the distance. Paul was about to switch on his ignition when he spotted Katie galloping with furious haste up the rocky slope towards him. She brought Nero right up to his buggy.

"Paul, he's been seen! On Pike Fell!" Without another word, she turned Nero and made off as she had come.

Paul turned on his walkie talkie to contact David. "Pike Fell!" he said briefly, before crunching into gear to set off after Katie. It was not long before he overtook her, riding like the wind towards Pike Fell. The buggy careered on up the steep stony track,

28

its wheels flinging out a cloud of pebbles and dust.

Quite oblivious to his danger, Jamie had stopped by a mountain stream to drink. He was completely exhausted after the long climb from his father's farm, but he felt safer up here, and it was time to think about his next move. He sank down on the sun-warmed rocks and gazed at the bubbling stream, pondering over the dog and their escape and getting back his breath.

"Don't you want to drink, boy?" he asked. "You must be thirsty....." The words died in his throat. Pierre was crouching low against the rocks, his eyes glowing like two red hot coals. Foam bubbled on his jaw and his teeth showed in a fearful yellow snarl.

"What's the matter, Pierre?" whimpered Jamie, backing against a rock. The dog rose on its hackles and advanced a pace, the hair on its back bristling.

"Pierre!" cried Jamie, suddenly terrified. "What is it . . .?" But there was no recognition in those mad eyes. Pierre's face was a contorted mask now — a thing out of some terrible nightmare. He advanced another pace. Trapped against the rocks, Jamie saw that dreadful mask loom closer and closer.

A voice cut in sharply. "Jamie! Don't move. Stay just where you are. When I say go — run!" Paul was standing on a rock, outlined against the sky, gripping his jacket in his hands.

"GO!" Jamie bolted sideways. Pierre, teeth bared, sprang after him. But before he could sink his fangs into Jamie's neck, Paul was on him, smothering him with the thick jacket. Jamie collided into a rock face and fell. In an awful daze he watched Paul roll beneath the frenzied creature's assault, saw him lose his grip on the protecting jacket, saw Pierre turn with frightful swiftness and open jaws.

A shot rang out — followed by a deathly hush. David stood above them, his rifle still aimed and smoking in his hands. The rabid dog lay still and dead before him.

Two days later David came in with a handful of post to find Paul jabbing painfully at the typewriter with two fingers. "Not one of your major talents, is it?" he remarked.

"What?" grunted Paul, absorbed in rubbing out another mistake.

"Typing," laughed David. He flung the post onto the table and began to open the local newspaper with a secret smile. "Oh, by the way, Katie looked in while you were out this morning. Wonders if you would like to go riding. She's got three horses of her own you know.''

Paul grimaced, "I'm not sure I would manage.''

"Course you would. It's a chance to get to know Katie better — besides, it would be useful for you to know how to ride.''

Grinning, Paul pushed the typewriter away. "Yes, I suppose so. Any sign of that lorry driver, by the way? The one who picked up that dog in France, I mean.''

"There won't be now, will there?'' said David. "Not with the story all over the papers!'' He opened the newspaper wide with a flourish — and there in the middle of the page was a picture of Paul, and an article headed YOUTH IN RABID DOG MOUNTAIN DRAMA.

"Oh heck, said Paul, pleased but a little embarrassed. He didn't know what else to say.

David just beamed down at him. "Not a bad start,'' he said, "to a Park Warden's career.''

At Scarsdale Farm, Katie was getting her riding tackle together. It was Susie's afternoon off and Margaret was busy shelling peas for supper at the kitchen table.

"Oh, you know Countess had a litter last month,'' she said, casually. Katie stopped at the door.

"At Barton's place, yes?''

"Five lovely pups,'' went on Margaret. She popped open a fat green pod and looked up at her daughter's expectant face. "I've just found a home for one of them as a matter of fact. Jamie's going to call him William!''

CHAPTER TWO

FUGITIVE

July had turned into August and still the heatwave continued. The whole countryside blistered under the scorching sun. High on the moors above Maltby a gang of convicts were working under guard. In the valley immediately below them lay Maltby Prison, a grey draggle of grim stone buildings which had housed French prisoners-of-war during Napoleon's time, and since then had become one of England's harshest and most dreaded prisons. Few had ever broken out of it, and of these even fewer had escaped across the open windswept moors that stretched as far as the eye could see in all directions. But Tommy Higgs had laid his plans well. Though he was known as a hardened criminal with an appalling record of violent crime behind him, he had kept his nose clean this time round in jail, and through good behaviour earned the right to go out with a working party. It was not long before he noted that the bread van into Eskdale went past the Quarry where he and his fellow prisoners worked at exactly ten o'clock every morning. He had saved up enough cigarettes, too, to bribe Johnno Briggs, a rough old lag who had spent ten years locked up, to help him in his scheme.

Now, as they slaved with pick and shovel in the blazing sun, he worked his way towards Johnno.

"One minute to go, Johnno," he hissed. Johnno went on swinging his pick.

"Use your loaf, son," he said quietly. "Another three years if you go steady, and you'll be out of here." Tommy struck the rocks in front of him a vicious blow.

"I caught a wild bird once, Johnno," he whispered. "Wild bird. I kept it in the house. Tried to tame it. Course it soon died. I mean, there are some things that can't stand being locked away, know what I mean? They just can't stand it. So I told you what I want you to do."

Johnno gave him a searching look. "Alright son," he muttered. "I'll do it." With that, he fell backwards with a sudden sharp cry of pain. He clutched his belly, writhing in agony, a trickle of blood running from the corner of his lips. The two prison guards ran to him, followed by the working party. Shriek after shriek of agony rent the air. As they clustered round the stricken man, Tommy leapt for the nearest rock and rolled over it out of sight. He fell into a deep gully and plummeted to the heather below, almost knocking the breath from his body. Then he was on his feet and running in great bounds from rock to rock, down the hillside, Johnno's shrieks growing dimmer and dimmer in his ears. Within minutes, the guards had restored order, lifted Johnno onto a hurdle and ordered four men to carry him away. By the time, they noticed Tommy's absence, he was half a kilometre away, and running as though his life depended on it for the road.

Tommy hid behind a loose stone wall, panting for breath. Far above him, he could see two minute figures in blue running down the hill towards his hiding place. But it would be ten minutes at least before they reached the road, and Tommy had timed things perfectly.

The bread van was even now labouring in bottom gear up the hill towards him. As it slowed down still further to round the corner, Tommy leapt for the back. The stone wall hid him from the driver's mirror, and the straining engine drowned any sound he made. He was a well built young man, as swift and light as a cat, and within moments he had gained the roof. Tommy hung on grimly as the van swung and lurched along the mountain lane. Twice he was almost flung off as it took a sudden bend. Once he had to shift his ground and hang precariously from the back as a lorry passed. At last, bruised, dusty, parched with thirst but triumphant, he dropped from the roof thirty kilometres from the prison, in the midst of Bearsdale.

Tommy trudged off through the heather until he came to a small brook. Gratefully, he drank deeply then straightened up to look about him. Far below lay a mountain farm. A woman was hanging out her washing and Tommy's lean face broke into a wolfish grin. He could not get far in his prison clothes, and here were clothes for the taking.

After a few minutes the woman disappeared into the house and Tommy moved in, creeping from rock to rock like a snake. Seconds later he had what he wanted — a blue cotton shirt and jeans. He stopped briefly to help himself to a loaf and a bottle of milk from the doorstep. Then he was away.

By nightfall, he was safe among the mountains. He changed his clothes, hiding his prison uniform under a pile of stones, gobbled down the loaf of bread, drank the milk, and smashed the empty bottle against the rocks. Finally, exhausted, he lay down among the heather and slept instantly.

The following day as they were finishing breakfast, Margaret and Katie heard Paul turn into the yard. Katie stuffed a piece of toast in her mouth and jumped up to meet him. Watching her go, Margaret could not help feeling a burst of pride. Katie looked so lovely in her boots and breeches and open necked shirt as she ran out. Margaret saw Paul thump her in friendly fashion as he climbed out of his buggy.

"Got the day off have you?" she called cheerily through the open door.

"Sort of," admitted Paul. "David's catching up on his paperwork. Told me I might as well get used to being on horseback."

"Meaning you want me to give you a lesson," laughed Katie. "Alright come and help me get them tacked up."

"I'll leave you to it," Margaret said. "I've got eleven calls to make this morning, and then Surgery! Have a good time — and don't fall off!" She was gone before Paul could think of anything suitably witty to say in reply.

"Who have you got for me today?" he asked, as he and Katie sauntered over to the stables.

"Lady," said Katie, collecting a bridle and saddle from the tack room.

"Lady?" groaned Paul, disappointed.

"What's wrong with Lady?"

"Nothing, she's just — well, she's a bit sedate."

"You're not exactly Harvey Smith yet," Katie laughed.

"Oh, I don't know," breezed Paul, full of confidence. "I thought I might have a go on Nero."

"You're not ready for Nero yet".

"How do you know until you let me try?" asked Paul. Katie looked at him, smiling in a curious way.

"All right, Nero it is," she said at last.

Soon afterwards, Paul and Katie were cantering

together across the moors below Pike Fell. They did not see Tommy sitting among the rocks above the valley. He had slept like a log and now, with the sun warming his back, he was taking it easy and working out his next move. The sound of horses thundering across the dry turf roused him. Leaping for cover behind a massive boulder, he peered down warily. Paul and Katie were mounting the slope towards him, not two hundred metres away.

"O.K.?" yelled Katie.

"Fine!" shouted Paul. "Nothing to it is there?"

"Keep him back!" Katie said, anxiously. "Don't let it turn into a race."

But Paul was getting a little too big for his boots. "Race you!" he cried, egging Nero into a gallop.

"No!" cried Katie. "You can't hold him!" But she was too late. Nero took the bit between his teeth and shot off, and Paul found that he was quite out of control. Horrified, he saw the heather rush by him at growing speed. A ditch loomed up across his path — somehow he cleared it, but another was upon him before he could regain his balance and he lost a stirrup. Furiously he hauled on the reins — he might just as well have tried to stop a runaway train. Now a stone wall was approaching. Paul had a brief vision of sky and stones and heather rotating above him, followed by the sound of a tremendous thump as he landed flat on his back. Nero veered off at an angle, fetched up against the wall and came to a halt, trembling. Before long, Paul became aware of a worried face bending over him.

"Are you all right?" Katie asked. He sat up with exaggerated care, his ears singing.

"You enjoyed that, didn't you?" he said crossly.

"I did warn you not to ride Nero," said Katie. "Hold Lady, while I catch him and take him home."

"What about me?" asked Paul, plaintively. Katie's temper snapped completely.

There's a road down there in the valley," she retorted. "You had better hitch home." From his hiding place, Tommy watched Katie mount Nero and lead Lady away.

He saw Paul stump off down to the road and chuckled to himself.

That afternoon, David returned from his rounds to find one extremely sulky boy scowling at the empty fireplace.

"The Wallaces have just phoned," Paul said. "They want us to call round and see to the fencing by the bridle path. A car's been into it without stopping and the sheep are getting through."

David sighed, "I'll see to it."

"They were pretty cross about another thing," added Paul morosely. "Somebody's stolen some of Jim Wallace's clothes from the line — and taken the morning's bread and milk off their doorstep."

"Hippies, perhaps," remarked David. "Dropouts they call them, don't they? Amazing how they drop in again once their tummies start rumbling."

Paul smiled wanly and, muttering something about coffee, walked as normally as he could manage into the kitchen.

David frowned. "You all right?"

"How do you mean?" said Paul defensively.

"I thought you were limping."

"I caught my foot, climbing a fence," said Paul shortly.

"I see," David dropped the subject and returned to his favourite pastime — lighting his pipe.

At Scarsdale Farm, Katie had untacked Nero and Lady and put them into their stables for the night. Now, just a little ashamed of herself, she was in the kitchen, filling the kettle. Suddenly she felt that someone was watching her. She swung round. A young man was leaning against the kitchen door. He was extremely good looking in a raffish way, with a shock of dark hair, and clear grey eyes, and white teeth which glinted clearly in his deeply bronzed face. His denim shirt left his tanned neck and arms bare and his blue jeans seemed a size too large.

"Hello, darlin'," he said easily. "I saw the brass plate. You the vet, then?"

"No," said Katie, slightly startled. "That's my mother. She's out at the moment, I'm afraid."

"You put people up, I see," said the young man. Katie nodded speechlessly in reply. "Anyone

stayin' at the moment?'' This time she shook her head. "Suits me.'' The young man strolled into the kitchen as if he owned it. "I like it quiet. My name's Mason, by the way, George Mason.'' Grinning broadly, he extended his hand.

"Katie Jackson,'' said Katie automatically. "How long do you want to stay?''

Tommy flung himself down onto the kitchen settle. "Oh a few days. I couldn't help seein' horses in the yard outside. Yours are they?''

Rather bemused, Katie sat down at the table opposite him. This young man absolutely radiated drive and personality — and so few people ever came to Bearsdale.

"Yes they're mine. I love horses,'' she said.

"Me too,'' smiled Tommy. "My dad was a jockey — one of the best. So I grew up with horses — wanted to be a jockey myself. By the time I was sixteen, I realised I wasn't goin' to make the weight.''

An hour later, Margaret came back from her rounds, to find a large young man sprawling across the kitchen table, eating an enormous omelette with a mug of coffee, his long legs thrust out in front of him. Katie was slicing bread.

"This is George,'' she told her mother. "George Mason. He's staying for a few days.''

Margaret studied Tommy while she unpacked her veterinary bag, and did not like what she saw. True, he was a handsome looking chap — the trouble was he clearly knew it, and exploited his obvious charm. She did not like the way he looked at Katie as she bustled around him, and still less did she like the way he had hardly bothered to greet her, as though he sensed her instant dislike and did not care.

"You Katie's ma?'' he grinned. Margaret thought she had never seen such a confident insolent grin in her life.

"That's right," she said icily.

"Glad to meet you," said Tommy, not bothering to get up or shake hands, just waving his fork in the air. "Me and Katie are just gettin' acquainted, like. Hope we'll get to know one another better soon."

Over at Grimsdyke, Paul was frying up some bacon and eggs. David could see that he was in poor spirits and wondered if he was overworking him.

"We needn't start work until ten tomorrow. Care for a ride with Katie first? I'm told your horsemanship is improving." This turned out to be exactly the wrong thing to say. Paul stumped off to the larder without a word.

"Out of bacon," he announced after a few minutes silence.

"Never mind," said David equably, getting out a couple of plates. "Just eggs will do me."

"Eggs it is then," mumbled Paul as he trailed back to the cooker. He broke them into the pan with undue force. "I think I'll skip riding with Katie for a few days. I've got a heck of a lot of paper work to catch up with — and I promised to whitewash this room."

****

It was way past ten o'clock when Susie came down to say Tommy would like tea in bed.

"Likes his comforts doesn't he?" remarked Margaret rather coolly. "Alright, Susie, take him some if he must have it. Here you are."

"Cheeky devil, he is!" laughed Susie on her way upstairs. "Asked me what I did in the evenings. Wait till I tell my fella!"

When she had gone, Margaret sat down next to Katie with her mug of tea. She frowned into the steaming brown liquid and then looked up determinedly at her daughter.

"Where does he come from?" she demanded.

"George?" asked Katie, apparently absorbed in the local paper. "I don't know really."

Margaret sipped her tea thoughtfully. "He hasn't any luggage. Has he got any money?"

Katie sighed and put down her paper. "I expect so," she said evenly. "He wouldn't be staying here otherwise would he? Anyway, he said he liked to travel light." There was a marked silence. "You don't like him do you?" She gave her mother an accusing glare and Margaret stood up stiffly and banged her mug on the table top.

"No, I don't," she said crisply. "I don't quite know why, but I don't — that's all. Perhaps its because I don't like his manners." In a matter of seconds she had picked up her appointments book and her medical bag and hurried out into the yard. Katie, a little startled by this reaction, watched her drive away.

"I'm off now until two," said Susie, clumping into the kitchen in her wellington boots. "Can you see to the phone till I'm back?"

"Yes, O.K.," murmured Katie, returning to her paper. There was a point-to-point in Scoresby next week, and she was soon lost in thought wondering whether Nero or Lady would carry her best after these weeks without rain. She was so absorbed that she did not hear Tommy creep in behind her.

Suddenly he was standing over her, the rifle that usually hung above the mantelpiece aimed at her startled face. He laughed at her expression and tossed the rifle from hand to hand. "Does it work?"

41

"What?"

"The gun, darlin!"

"Of course, it does."

Tommy sauntered across to the table. "Do you ever use it?" he asked casually.

"Only when we have to," she replied in surprise.

"You don't hunt then?"

"No," said Katie decisively, "I don't like killing things."

"Way of nature though, isn't it," grinned Tommy. He squinted down the rifle sight and aimed at a jug of flowers on the window sill. "Red in tooth and claw."

"Animals only kill for food, not for pleasure," Katie retorted. There was a pile of washing-up sitting in the sink and she began to stack things up, grateful for the diversion. Fascinating though he was, there was something about George that faintly disturbed her.

"Oh I don't know," said Tommy easily. "I've seen a cat play with a mouse." He stretched luxuriously and spread out his feet. "Built up the place from scratch, did you?"

"Well, when Dad died there was a little money — not much. Mum built up her practise here as a vet and I — well, I just went to school and started taking people out on the moors at weekends and school hols when we began to let rooms here. I bought Nero three years ago, and Bonny a few months back."

Tommy whistled. "You must be rollin' in it!"

"Wish I was! No, I made some money working at Colonel Ransom's stables on Saturdays. And some of it came from a savings fund, and the rest from the bank — mum borrowed it for me. I still haven't paid her back though."

Tommy hung the rifle back on its mountings. "I love horses. Any chance of exercisin' them for you while I'm here?"

"Can you ride then?"

He laughed, "I told you darlin', my dad was a jockey. Was out with horses since I was so high."

Katie wiped away a wisp of hair with soapy hands and turned to look at him. "I'd be glad of the help — if you know what you're doing."

"Oh, I know what I'm doin' alright. In fact, I fancy a go on the big hunter."

"Nero!" exclaimed Katie. "He can be a pig."

"That's because he's so proud. He won't take nothin' from nobody. I like that."

Katie laughed and glanced round and her heart missed a beat. Tommy was sitting on the table grinning broadly at her. His eyes were such a strange penetrating blue they seemed to be boring right through her. This won't do, she thought, laughing inwardly at her fancy. I must say something casual.

"What do you do for a living?"

Tommy wiggled his long fingers in the air. "I'm handy. Can turn my hand to almost anythin'. Usually do. Jack of all trades, I am."

"Are you now?" said Katie, smiling. "Like to come out with me this morning. We'll see what you're made of on horseback." Tommy grinned back at her, his blue eyes, sparkling now.

"O.K. darlin'. You're on."

Half an hour later found Katie and Tommy out together on the rough moors that stretched beneath the southern slopes of Thorpes Ridge. Katie quickly discovered that Tommy could certainly ride. He sat Lady easily, like one born to the saddle. As they turned into a canter he neither pulled at his mount nor flogged her on, but moved smoothly into the lead, guiding Lady with a light hand. She, recognising an experienced rider in the saddle, went like the wind, pacing Nero with thundering hooves across the lonely windswept expanses of heather that led up to the ridge, until at last the two snorting horses were brought in.

"You can certainly ride," admitted Katie, puffing for breath. "I'll give you a go on Nero tomorrow if you like."

"You're on, darlin'," said Tommy. Then he was off again, sending Lady swiftly along the narrow stony track. Katie whooped aloud with excitement, wheeled Nero about and chased after him. Together they cleared two loose stone walls in rapid succession and galloped on up the hillside.

Paul, out on his rounds, saw them from his beach buggy speeding towards him across the heather. He stopped to look and they cantered up to him.

"Open the gate will you, Paul!" called Katie. Paul did as he was told and they went through. He closed the gate and watched them thunder off into the distance. Then frowning, he drove off to Scarsdale Farm.

Margaret was in the surgery when Paul arrived. A very old man was holding his sheepdog on the surgery table while Margaret made an injection. "Steady, Bill," she soothed. "Easy! I'm not hurting you." Swabbing the spot, she spoke to the old man. "He'll be fine in a couple of days. Keep up the pills, and let me know how he gets on will you?"

"Aye, I will," he grunted. He gave Bill a loud whistle and the dog sprang from the table and followed the old man out of the surgery. Margaret washed her hands carefully at the sink.

"Who's that Katie's out with today," asked

Paul casually.

"Oh, that's George." She grimaced as she dried her hands. "He's staying here for a few days. Rides well, does he?"

"Yes," said Paul, without expression. Margaret glanced at him and felt a pang of compassion. He looked so forlorn standing there with his denim cap in his hand, and his freckled face full of concern. Margaret was not blind, she could see how impressed Katie was with George and she knew that Paul was being left out in the cold. George had experience, looks and charm when he felt like it, but for some reason she could not quite explain, Margaret liked Paul vastly better, and she was sorry to see him looking so down in the dumps.

"Care to come to supper tonight?" she asked. "I know David's going to be out this evening."

Paul straightened and pulled at his cap. "Thanks, but I've got a lot of paper work to catch up on." Before Margaret could try to persuade him he was gone. She watched him tear off in his garish beach buggy and sighed.

Later that afternoon, Margaret and Susie went into Scoresby village leaving Tommy lounging on the sofa with the papers, waiting for Katie to serve him his afternoon tea. "Nice here," he said lazily. "You know, I've a mind to settle down in Bearsdale."

"Live here you mean?"

"Yeah, why not? I daresay I could get a job. I can turn my hands to most things — and its peaceful. Who was that chap who opened the gate by the way?"

"Oh, that's Paul — Paul Graham. He's one of the wardens."

Tommy's heart lurched but he spoke quite

easily. "The Fuzz you mean?"

"Good lord, no," laughed Katie. "This is all part of Bearsdale National Park. The Wardens, well they sort of run the place. Conservation, and that sort of thing."

Inwardly, he breathed a sigh of relief. "Oh, I see. Friend of yours is he?"

"I know him slightly," said Katie coolly. "He's O.K. — just a bit young." She wandered off to the larder to find some more sugar and Tommy chuckled and went back to his paper. Suddenly he froze. It was not a particularly noticeable paragraph in the paper, but it was enough to alarm him very much indeed. Headed, *'Hiker makes find,'* it went on *'A climber near Pike Fell found prison clothing belonging to Tommy Higgs, who escaped from a prison working party three days ago.'* Tommy did not read any further. He was on his feet in a flash, moving to the fireplace. He took down the rifle and checked the breech. Empty. Looking about him his eyes found the Welsh dresser and he pulled open the drawers. Nothing. His glance fell on the bureau where Margaret kept her papers. Moving to it swiftly, he found it unlocked and began to search frantically among the letters and files. Right at the back was a small box of bullets. Smiling to himself, Tommy pocketed the box just as Katie returned with the sugar and a large tin of biscuits. He watched her as she made the tea things ready, clattering spoons and cups on to a tray.

"Fancy another ride later, darlin'?" he asked.

"You're keen, aren't you?" laughed Katie, moving to the stove.

"Keen as mustard, darlin'." He was grinning, but his eyes were as cold and watchful as a snake's.

Unaware of the drama beginning to unfold at

Scarsdale, Paul was sitting in the office, miserably pecking away at the typewriter when David breezed in through the door. "Try using more fingers," he suggested. Paul was not amused and went on battering away on the keyboard. "Why don't you take a bit of time off when you've finished that?" said David, "It is your day off, after all."

"I might, I'll see."

"Go out with Katie — get a breath of fresh air."

"She's a bit busy at present."

"I see," said David. Like Margaret he understood very well what was going on at Scarsdale. Paul continued to attack the typewriter crossly, so David turned his attention to the afternoon's mail. The phone rang.

"Bearsdale National Park," he said cheerily, then he frowned. "Sergeant Morris! Yes sure, I'll tell our people to keep their eyes open. Posters, sure. Send me a dozen over right away and I'll put them about. No sign of the chap, I suppose. Sounds a tough customer. Hope you lay hands on him soon." He rang off and turned to Paul. "Looks as though we've got a runaway criminal on our hands! Remember that chap Tommy Higgs who broke out from a working party in Maltby? He's at large here in Bearsdale. Apparently it was in the national press this morning but it's the first I've heard of it!"

Paul stopped typing. "He must be holed up somewhere. Hadn't we better ring round the hill farms?"

"Yes, I think we had better — beginning with Scarsdale. You never know. They might have caught sight of him."

****

Katie was watching the telly, with her feet up and a

47

magazine spread over her lap. Upstairs, Tommy was taking a bath and Katie was revelling in the peace and comfort after another gruelling ride across the moors. She was watching the Cross Country event at Badminton. Horse after horse plunged into view, some refusing the tall fences, others taking them well and galloping on. There were two or three spectacular falls. Katie fell to thinking what it would be like to take part in such a punishing and risky event. She could imagine George taking this course too.

She must have dozed off for a few minutes for she was jerked awake by some rousing music heralding the early evening news. The announcer droned on and on and her eyelids began to droop again. Another item began. "Prison clothing believed to belong to Thomas Higgs, who escaped from Maltby High Security Prison three days ago, has been found in Bearsdale National Park. Extra police are being drafted into the area and a full scale search is being organised. The following picture of Higgs was put out today . . ." Katie sat forward rigid with horror as George's picture flashed up on the screen. "If you have seen this man," continued the announcer, "You should get in touch with the nearest police station at once. A police spokesman today warned the public against tackling Higgs. He is violent and highly dangerous."

"Now isn't that a shame!" Katie leapt round to see Tommy standing in the doorway. "Real shame that is, your gettin' to know about me like this. Just when we were gettin' cosy," he said grinning. Katie sprang for the phone but Tommy was there before her. With a quick movement he yanked out the flex. "Now we had better decide what to do with you," he hissed. An ugly leer came over his face. "Can't have you lettin' on to the police, can we?"

David was dialling Margaret's number for the third time. "Still getting unobtainable?" asked Paul.

"Must be out of order," said David. "I wonder if I should nip over there? Let them know about this Higgs."

Paul jumped to his feet. "I'll go!"

"Alright. Might give you the chance you've been waiting for." He smiled through his pipe smoke at Paul's puzzled face. "To make it up with Katie!"

By now, Tommy had taken full control of the situation and was loading the rifle. Katie shrank back against the Welsh dresser, her face as white as the plates behind her.

"Why don't you just take what you want and go?" she whispered.

"That's what I'm goin' to do, darlin'," said Tommy, flashing his infectious grin. Only now the grin was tinged with menace. "I'm goin' to collect some cash and shoot off — only you're comin' with me in case of trouble." At that moment Katie heard Paul's buggy turn into the yard. She lunged for the window, but Tommy was there before her blocking the way.

"Get rid of him. Remember what they said on the telly, I'm dangerous darlin'. Likely to be violent."

Paul hopped out of his buggy and ran up to the front door. He was not sure what sort of reception he would get from Katie, and he took a deep breath before knocking. Katie opened the door almost immediately.

"Yes?" she said coldly.

"Hello, Katie," he gabbled as cheerfully as he could muster. "I just called to let you know your phone's out of order."

"We know, thanks."

"Oh, by the way, there's a chap at large in Bearsdale, escaped from a working party. They've asked us to look out for him."

"Yes, I know," said Katie rudely.

"Don't worry, we'll look out for him." But his assurances were lost on her as she shut the door in his face. Stunned by her atrocious behaviour, he remained standing there for a moment. Then he turned sharply on his heels and went back to the beach buggy, red with anger and embarrassment.

As he drove off, Tommy emerged from behind the door with the rifle in his hand. He swept it round the room. "Good, girl. Any notes in the house?"

"Notes?" Katie asked stupidly.

Tommy raised his rifle a fraction, "Money, cash, darlin'." Hardly knowing how her legs managed it, she moved to the bureau.

"There might be a few pounds."

"Get 'em — and saddle up the horses."

Paul returned to Grimsdyke in a black mood to find David sorting posters into neat piles. Without a word, he flung himself onto the sofa.

"Any luck?" asked David.

"No, she would hardly speak to me," said Paul.

"Well, a bit of work will take your mind off things," said David cheerfully. "I want you to take some of these posters round." Paul took a pile and rose to go, then stopped, riveted to the spot. He had looked at the posters for the first time, and there was the man he knew as George.

****

The crags above Scarsdale shone golden in the sinking sun as Tommy gazed down into the peaceful valley. There was no sign of pursuit. He wheeled

Nero about to where Katie sat Lady.

"Why can't you just let me go!" she pleaded for the fourth time since they left the farm.

"No fear!" smiled Tommy. "I'm not going to risk your gettin' away — I need a hostage in case of trouble. Now MOVE!" He turned Nero and made off, breaking swiftly into a hard canter. Lady was used to following Nero and Tommy knew it. Within moments the riders were speeding along the ridge together.

Katie would never forget the next frightening half hour, as they dashed up steep grassy banks, across rushing streams and along high barren ridges. Jolted, breathless and terribly scared, she could only put her knees in and pray.

Meanwhile, David and Paul were racing down the road towards Scarsdale.

"What are we going to do?" demanded Paul. "He must be in the house with her!"

"Look," said David. "I've notified the police — I've told them what's happening. They're on their way but we'll be there before them. We'll just have to play it by ear."

Suddenly, Paul gave a cry. "There they are!" Far away, two people on horseback were flying over the hillside. Unknown to Tommy, he had taken a long route towards Grimsdyke and Katie was certainly not going to warn him about it. It had seemed her last chance.

David wrenched the wheel over and took the landrover through a gap in the stone walls that lined the mountain fields. "Hold on!" Paul needed no telling as David drove the tough vehicle headlong across the broken ground. They splashed heavily through two shallow streams, the tyres churning up loose stones and clouds of spray, only to charge

51

straight down through a flock of sheep, the poor beasts scattering at their approach. The landrover was gaining on the riders rapidly, and neither Tommy nor Katie had spotted them — yet.

"We'll cut them off here," David shouted above the roar of the engine. He brought the vehicle round, tyres spinning in the stony ground, and thrashed over the grass towards the end of the ridge. They turned sharply — so sharply that Paul was nearly thrown out. He recovered himself with an effort. The door next to him had flown open and he had just managed to shut it before a really huge jolt almost threw him through the roof.

They were charging downhill now, and Paul

could see Tommy and Katie riding straight towards them. The riders saw the landrover homing in on them and turned aside, but David was quicker. Spinning the wheel in his powerful hands, he swung the landrover and charged down between them. Nero bolted uphill and Lady went off to the left, met a deep stream, lost her footing and fell heavily. Katie was thrown clear. As she tottered to her feet, bruised and muddy, she saw Lady find her feet and plunge away, the landrover coming to a halt and then Paul and David leaping out and running towards her. David got to her first while Paul grabbed Lady's reins.

"I'm all right!" gasped Katie, but there was blood on her chin and a nasty bruise on her forehead. Without a word, Paul mounted Lady, turned her towards where Tommy had vanished over the top of the ridge and made off at full gallop after him. David helped Katie into the landrover and within moments he too had joined the pursuit.

Paul was riding as he had never done before. The ground was cracked and treacherous and Lady threatened to come down at any moment. But Paul was heedless of the risk he ran. He was only conscious of a burning rage as he drove Lady over the rocky slope. Then he saw Tommy turn to look behind him as he sped on ahead. It was a mistake, for at that moment Nero stumbled, and Tommy was thrown heavily to the ground. The convict was on his feet in a moment. He had lost the rifle in the fall, but now he seized a broken branch from the ground and swung it viciously at Paul as he galloped up. Lady plunged violently and Paul, too, came off.

In a dreadful daze, he watched Tommy grin wolfishly and come at him, swinging the great branch. Just in time he rolled aside and heard

Tommy's blow hit the rock behind him with terrible force. Tommy took a swift step backwards and swung again, but before he could attack a quiet voice cut in.

"I wouldn't do that if I were you." It was David standing by his landrover with Katie, wide-eyed, beside him, and Tommy's rifle at the ready.

****

The following morning, David was hard at work in his office, writing a report on the capture of Higgs. Margaret looked in on her way back from her rounds.

"Hi!" she called.

"Hi," said David morosely, chewing at his pen for inspiration.

"What's the matter with you?" asked Margaret.

"Don't like paper work," he grumbled.

"I thought you were leaving all that to Paul."

David stopped chewing and grinned at her. "About time I did my share."

"Where is Paul, anyway?" demanded Margaret.

"Out riding with Katie, didn't you know?" replied David, and his eyes twinkled with laughter. "Paul may not ride as well as that other chap, but I think Katie realises that he's the better man."

CHAPTER THREE

CONTEST

It was weeks since the excitement of Tommy Higgs' escape had shattered the peace and quiet of Bearsdale National Park. Since then, little more had happened than a herd of cows escaping onto the main highway through the Park and the usual small grumbles, problems and complaints from the hill farmers to worry the Warden and his new assistant.

Today they were kiting from Thorpes Ridge. The huge hang-gliders, gaily coloured orange, yellow, scarlet and blue, soared gracefully against the bright summer sky. On the ridge itself, a row of vehicles, ranging from ancient Fords to a battered beach buggy was parked close to the edge and young people in fluorescent overalls were setting up their kites. Among them was Paul. He had got together all his savings and passed the training course with flying colours. Now he was the proud possessor of a splendid orange hang-glider and, when the wind allowed, went kiting at every opportunity. There was to be a contest next Saturday and Paul was determined to get in as much practice as he possibly could.

George, the stocky, bearded young man who ran the local gliding club, came bustling up. "Ready!" he bellowed against the wind. Paul gave a thumbs up for George to lift the bows of his kite and broke into a lumbering run. For a few moments he was staggering under a heavy burden, then miraculously the weight lightened as the kite lifted him into the air. There was a sickening moment as the ground fell away beneath him. The kite dipped suddenly and Paul held his breath, but as the kite gained height above the valley floor, it gained lift. He soared on upwards, turned gently as he rose on the air current and dipped slightly to avoid two kites sweeping towards him. Then he lifted with the wind towards the distant peaks.

On the moorland road, far below, two people were watching his progress from their gleaming open-topped sports car. They were brother and sister, both in their twenties, both extremely good-looking and both clad identically in expensive denim suits and brightly checked shirts. Gail and Kenny Deverell were very much out of the 'top drawer.' Their father, a successful Californian businessman, was now with the State Department in London, and his children were accustomed to the best of everything.

Kenny was a pleasant easy-going young man with Harvard and Law School written all over him. Everyone liked this modest, hard working boy — unlike his sister who was not so popular among their wide circle of friends. Spoilt, restless and difficult, Gail demanded instant attention wherever she went. She was always trying new experiences in order to fill the emptiness in her life. Yachting, car racing, show jumping — she had tried them all, and insisted that Kenny should try them too. For in her way she was devoted to her shy hulk of a brother, and had come to believe that she and Kenny should always stand together against the hostile and very unpredictable world they lived in.

Hang gliding was her latest fad and she had dragged Kenny, somewhat against his will, up to Bearsdale which was reputed to have the best hang gliding in England, so that they could take part in the big Bank Holiday Rally; Gail was quite determined that Kenny should win.

"That kid's good," observed Kenny, squinting at Paul through his binoculars.

"Not in your class," Gail sneered.

"He can certainly handle a kite."

"Wait until the contest," said Gail, putting the clutch in. "That usually separates the men from the boys." The powerful car shot off in a cloud of dust.

Paul was soaring happily above the valley. The only sound was a gentle rustle of air on the kite. From his vantage point, high in the sky, he could see three kites in the distance and beyond, the mountains of the Border lying range after range into the distant horizon. Below lay a criss-crossed pattern of tiny stone-walled fields, with flocks of minute sheep and dotted here and there a lonely hill farm.

He began to think about the Rally. It would be a big event. Scores of kiters would be coming from all over England and even from abroad. Katie would be coming too. How he wished he could persuade her to take up kiting with him . . .

A powerful down draught caught him completely unawares. The kite dipped sharply. Paul tried to correct the fall, but he still had a lot to learn. Before he could gain control and lift, the kite was falling, falling, steadily into the valley. The wind chose this moment to fail and he lost even more height. A little church loomed up in front of him. Generations of Dalesmen had come from the surrounding hill farms to worship there, and from its square tower men had once kept watch against the invading Scots. Now

Paul had to turn abruptly to avoid storming it himself, and in doing so lost still more height. Realising that he had to make a landing, he steadied himself and looked out for a suitable spot. A large field came into sight. He just managed to clear the stone wall that bounded it when to his horror he saw that he was heading straight for a flock of sheep.

There was no avoiding them. The sheep stampeded as Paul came whistling in over their heads. Then, with a slight shock, he was down. He started to unhook his harness, but as he did so he became uncomfortably aware of a furious old man stumping across the field towards him, waving a thick stick. His face, weathered by sixty years in the open air, resembled a withered apple. In spite of the warm sun, he wore a shapeless tweed hat, a raincoat tied with

string, corduroy trousers and heavy boots that had seen better days. The name of this apparition was Elijah, and he was the most cantankerous hill farmer in the whole of Bearsdale, which was quite a reputation to hold.

"Ey!" he yelled. "What the dickens do you think yer playin' at, eh?"

"Sorry," said Paul.

"Sorry!" stormed Elijah, waving his stick in Paul's astonished face. "Sorry! You nearly kill my best ewes and yer sorry!"

"It was an accident." Elijah took no notice.

"Call yourself a Warden? Your job's to protect the livestock round 'ere — not frighten it 'alf to death!"

"I'm very sorry but it was an accident, really."

"Aye!" Well, we'll just have to see what yer boss has to say about that, won't we?" The old farmer stumped off, muttering loudly under his breath. Paul picked up the kite and braced himself for the long trudge back up to Thorpes Ridge. He had an idea that there would be trouble about this and he was right.

****

"Right on Elijah's sheep!" exploded Katie. "It must have been terribly funny!"

She was sitting by the kitchen table, mending a torn pair of jeans, while Margaret ironed a pile of shirts. The housework had been mounting up while Susie was away, visiting relations in London.

"I expect Elijah's furious," Margaret said.

"He is. He's going to take proceedings against the hang-gliding people — at least that's what Paul said when he phoned."

"Well, they have a point," said Margaret thoughtfully.

"They have to practice somewhere!" Katie muttered through a mouthful of pins. "The Bank Holiday Rally happens next weekend — and Paul's tipped to win it." The phone rang and Margaret set down the iron to answer it.

"Jacksons . . . Oh heck! How did he do that?"

It was at this moment that Gail and Kenny arrived at Scarsdale Farm. Open mouthed, Gail took in the weathered farmhouse, the dilapidated barns and the battered Rangerover standing in the yard. "This is where we're staying?" she asked incredulously.

"This is it," said Kenny, moving round to the boot for their luggage.

"What a dump!"

"Take it easy!" Kenny exclaimed. "You're here to unwind remember."

Inside, Margaret was still on the phone. "Can he move? Well, keep him quiet — I'll be with you in half an hour." She rang off. "Blast!"

"What's up?" asked Katie.

"I'll have to go over to Colonel Ransom's place — one of his horses has had a nasty fall." As she hurried to the door, Kenny and Gail came in.

"Hi!" said Kenny brightly. "I'm Kenny Deverell, and this is my sister Gail. We're here for the kiting."

"Oh yes!" exclaimed Margaret. "We were expecting you. Sorry I can't stay, but I'm out on a call — Katie here will look after you."

"Fine," said Kenny as Margaret left. He turned his pleasant smile on Katie. "Nice place you have here — looks really old, if you know what I mean."

"Yes, it dates back a bit," said Katie. "As a

matter of fact . . ."

"I'll go run a bath," Gail cut in rudely. "There is a bath, I suppose?"

"Yes, upstairs," said Katie, too surprised to make any other comment. Gail had disappeared before she could collect her thoughts and there followed an awkward pause.

"Lovely countryside you've got around here," Kenny blurted out at last. "We should have a great time here, I think."

"Are you over here on holiday?" asked Katie.

"No," said Kenny. "We live in London. Dad's in the Diplomatic Service."

"I see," said Katie, ironically. Gail obviously had none of her father's diplomatic ability!

Upstairs, Gail viewed the bathroom with growing horror. It was perfectly clean, but the bath itself was at least fifty years old and the boiler looked even older. She had to light the thing with matches. There was a loud muffled thump which made her jump, and then the ancient boiler began to shake and wheeze asthmatically. Gail undressed and wrapped herself in a towelling bath robe before testing the water. It was stone cold and showed no signs of getting any warmer.

"Blast this place!" she swore to no-one in particular. "Why did we ever come here?"

David and Paul had breakfasted early at Grimsdyke, the following day, and Paul was now clearing away while David stowed a bundle of papers into his tattered briefcase.

"Ruddy meetings," he exclaimed. "I used to love London — now I can't wait to get out of it."

"When will you be back?" asked Paul as he started to stack their plates and mugs into a precarious pyramid on the draining board.

"Sunday, if I can."

"Oh, you'll miss the kiting," said Paul, disappointed.

"Sorry about that," said David. "I would love to have seen it. Good luck, anyway."

"Thanks," said Paul. He dived for a plate that had somehow dislodged itself from the pyramid and missed.

"If you could manage not to break your neck at least!" David laughed as Paul scooped up the fragments. "We're rather short staffed at the moment."

Paul chuckled. "I'll keep it in mind."

"Oh there was one thing you might sort out for me while I'm away. One of the hill farmers has been trying to get hold of me. I haven't the time to return his call. You might drop round there, find out what's going on. Elijah Jones is his name. Says a kite landed on his sheep of all things. Sort it out, will you? He's not a bad bloke really, when you get to know him."

At Scarsdale Farm, breakfast was not going so smoothly. Gail had come down late and in a filthy temper. She was used to city life, and the quiet country night had made her sleep badly. There was not enough hot water for the bath she was used to having each morning, and then the coffee was not to her taste and the bacon not crisp enough. Margaret was glad to shoot off on her rounds, while Kenny escaped the thunderous atmosphere to tinker with his much loved car. So Gail and Katie were left alone together. Gail lit a cigarette — her fifth since getting up.

"Is there anything to do here? Besides kiting, I mean?"

"Yes, lots," replied Katie. "Do you ride?"

"Horseback? No — I used to, but I find it a bit

62

dull after kiting.''

"I see," said Katie, looking at her spoilt face. She was beginning to get very irritated with Gail.

Gail was exhaling a long plume of smoke. "You must feel buried alive here."

"Not at all," said Katie evenly. "As a matter of fact, the only place I feel like that is London." Unfortunately, Gail was not used to being answered back, particularly by a 'country bumpkin' like Katie.

"Excuse me, won't you," she snapped. "I'm going to take a brisk walk." Paul walked in at that moment, and Gail pushed past him without even a glance.

"Who was that?" enquired Paul.

"Oh, that's Miss America," giggled Katie. "Gail Deverell. She and her brother are here for the contest."

"I see!" Paul sat down on the table and pinched a slice of toast from Katie's plate. "Look are you busy?" he asked between munches.

"Yes, but go on."

"I wondered if you would care for a spin in the buggy. I need some moral support."

Elijah was engaged in the tricky process of shifting his flock to another field when Paul and Katie drew up.

"If I'm not back in five minutes," said Paul, one hand on the gate. "Call the Police!" He advanced warily to the top of the field where Elijah was rounding up his flock. "Morning, Elijah!" he called, bracing himself for the storm.

"Jones to you," said Elijah, ominously.

"You wanted a word with me, I understand," stammered Paul. He kept one eye on the gate in case of a necessary escape — and the other on Timber, Elijah's mangy sheep dog who was peering nastily up at him.

"Not with you," grunted Elijah.

"David's away, I'm afraid."

"Is 'e now?" Elijah growled, even more ominously. "When's 'e due back then?"

"Sunday."

"That will do," said Elijah, unmoving.

"You're sure there's nothing that I can do?"

"You could go away," said Elijah. Timber snarled, baring his teeth, and advanced on Paul. At that point, Paul decided it was probably time to go.

"Tell yer friends with them damned gliders to watch it!" yelled Elijah as Paul half walked, half ran down the field. "If they land near my sheep again I'll set Timber on them! And that applies to you, too!"

"Well?" asked Katie, when Paul had reached the safety of his buggy.

"Oh, nothing to it," said Paul, breezily, although he was unusually silent all the way back to Scarsdale.

That afternoon, as they prepared to go out kiting, Gail said to Katie, "I suppose kiting is too risky for you?"

"Like horse riding for you, perhaps?" Katie retorted. She was smiling but staring very directly at Gail.

"Come on," said Kenny, hastily. He was a good-natured lad and resented the edge on his sister's voice when she spoke to Katie. "There's a good wind from the south! We'll miss it if we hang about."

"Riding today, are we?" asked Gail, glaring at Katie.

"Yes, on Kite's Ledge," said Katie, glaring back. "I expect I'll see you kiting."

64

"I expect I'll see you too," said Gail unpleasantly. An idea was beginning to form in her mind.

****

A brisk wind was blowing off Thorpe's Ridge. Kenny made ready for take off, watched by Gail and Paul close by.

"It's just not fair," Gail remarked to her companion. "The way Kenny is always the best." Kenny took off and soared effortlessly into the air. He dodged neatly as another kite crossed his path, took advantage of the updraught to gain height, and then settled down to hitting the target — an enormous canvas circle, bright orange, set up in the valley below. This was Kenny's last chance to practice before the Rally. He shifted his weight a little and dropped towards the target.

"He's losing too much height," exclaimed Gail. "Come on Kenny! You can make it, I know!"

"He's down!" said Paul. Kenny had landed six metres short of the target.

"Blast!" hissed Gail. To Paul's amazement, she was gripping her kite tightly and trembling with rage.

"Next!" called George. Without a word, Gail hooked herself in and took off. The wind lifted her powerfully and she flew exulting in the rising air. Then she spotted a minute figure on horseback racing across the heather. She laughed aloud, shifted her weight and plummeted like a hawk on its prey.

Cantering over the Ledge, Katie did not see Gail until it was too late. There was a loud whistling noise, and Gail's kite came at her from above like the Angel of Death. Nero was used to tractors and traffic but he had never met anything like this falling out of the sky. He put his head down and bolted.

Taken totally unawares, Katie had a brief view of the ground and sky wheeling about her. Then all went blank. When she came to, she found herself lying on the sofa at home. Margaret and Paul were with her, and her back ached very badly.

"Keep still," said Margaret with professional calm.

"What happened?" groaned Katie.

"You had a fall, remember?" Paul said gently.

"Oh yes," she said, trying to rise. "Where's Nero?"

"He's all right," said Paul. He pushed her firmly back down. "A chap found him and phoned me — I took him home."

Kenny came into the room at that moment, followed by Gail. "How are you?" he asked, full of concern.

"I'm fine," said Katie. "Just a bit shaken."

"And what the hell do you think you were playing at!" exploded Paul, catching sight of Gail in the background. "I said, what do you think you were up to!" He was quite beside himself with rage. "It's a miracle she wasn't killed!"

"I didn't know he would spook so easily," she replied, calmly. She was lying and Paul knew it — though he could never prove it, he knew. This made him even more furious.

"Spook!" he yelled. "Can you imagine what a kite must look like to a horse, coming straight at it?"

"All right, all right," snapped Gail petulantly, almost as angry now as Paul. "You've made your point."

"I'm glad I have," said Paul coldly. "Goodnight, Mrs Jackson." He stalked out without another word. Margaret helped Katie off the sofa.

"Upstairs, young lady. I'm going to put you to bed."

"I'm all right," protested Katie.

"No, you're not," she said firmly. "Bed."

After they had gone, Kenny looked accusingly at Gail, who examined her nails uncomfortably.

"I simply don't believe it!" she said defensively. "A brother of mine to just stand there and let that — that lug, talk to me like that."

Kenny's gaze was very cold. "What do you expect? If he hadn't said it I would have said it myself."

"Only you didn't say it — he did!" said Gail hotly. "And you let him! I want to go back to London — tonight."

"Not until after the contest tomorrow."

Gail turned on him like a tigress. "I said tonight!" But Kenny was not to be bullied this time.

"What's the matter Gail? Scared of facing them again tomorrow?"

"You must be joking!" she spat at him.

"Then we stay," said Kenny icily. "And when Mrs Jackson comes down you'll apologise." At that moment, Margaret came down the stairs. "How is Katie?" he asked.

"She'll be all right," said Margaret, equably. "She's had falls before, you know."

"I believe my sister has something to say to you," he went on, looking at Gail and waiting expectantly.

At last, Gail spoke. "I'm sorry about what happened." There was no expression in her voice at all.

"Well no harm done, thank goodness," said Margaret, lightly.

"I'm going to have a bath now, if you don't mind," Gail declared with a toss of her head. "That is, if there's any hot water." Kenny watched her go, then turned to Margaret, deeply embarrassed.

"I'm sorry about all this," he said. "You must try to understand about Gail." Margaret simply looked at him. "She's been under a big strain lately," he continued hastily, "That's why we came here really, to give her a break. You see, she was always a bit — well a bit neurotic. When our mother left us a year back, well — we were all upset, but Gail took it really hard. She seemed to think it was her fault — in fact she pretty well nearly had a breakdown. We thought if she came here, with lots of rest and exercise, and nothing to worry about . . ." His voice tailed off lamely.

"I understand," said Margaret quietly. "I know how these things are — and I'm glad you told me about it. I'm sure we can help."

"Oh, you've been great!" exclaimed Kenny, more embarrassed by her sympathy than ever. "I was just trying to explain." Margaret smiled, she felt sorry for Kenny and wanted very much to make things easier for him.

"Would you like a cup of real English tea? she asked.

"Great!" said Kenny, glad to have got everything off his chest. Margaret put the kettle on and began to lay out cups and saucers.

"I believe you're one of the stars of the show tomorrow."

"I'm in it, yes."

"Do you think you'll win?" she asked.

Kenny laughed and shrugged his shoulders. "With Paul in it, I would say it's wide open myself."

****

As soon as he thought it a reasonable hour of the morning, Paul rang to see how Katie was faring.

"I'm fine!" said Katie. "Just a few bruises, that's all. No, I haven't got concussion! Stop fussing! Yes, of course I'm going to the contest — wouldn't miss it for anything. I was wondering if you could pick me up on your way."

Gail and Kenny trooped downstairs just as she set down the receiver.

"Hello!" Kenny said, awkwardly. "You feeling O.K?"

"Fine," said Katie, beaming sunnily up at him— she could never harbour a grudge for long. "Paul's picking me up in a moment. I wouldn't miss the kiting for anything." She ran upstairs for her boots, taking two steps at a time. Kenny went into the kitchen and poured coffee for two.

"Filthy stuff!" exclaimed Gail, after one tentative sip. "Why can't they make coffee in England?"

Kenny put down his cup. "Gail. Do you have to find fault with everything? Do you have to be so unpleasant to everyone? These people are doing their best to make us feel at home."

"They're just hicks."

"No, they're country people — that's not the same thing. Gail, we came here because you need to unwind. The whole point is to take it easy."

Gail's nostrils flared angrily and her eyes narrowed. "Are you saying I'm some sort of nut?" Alarmed at her reaction, Kenny seized her by the arms.

"No, I'm saying you need a rest. Stop pushing people around, Gail. They want to be friends." Gail pushed him away.

"I don't care if they're friends or not! And I'll

tell you another thing, Kenny. I'm not going to have any of these people winning this contest. You're going to win Kenny — I mean that.''

****

The people of Bearsdale did not normally go in for display, but the Bank Holiday Rally was a general excuse to really let themselves go. Expensive sports cars, some of them with foreign number plates, stood next to the worn Fords and Landrovers belonging to the men and women of Bearsdale. There was a military band, ice-cream and balloons for the children, and even a fortune-teller who had set up her stall at a corner of the field. But the centre of attraction was, of course, the kites — twenty splendid hang-gliders lined up along the ridge.

Paul and Katie strolled along the line. ''That's Lawson,'' said Paul, ''He came first at Skipton last year. Schwartz, from West Germany. Nice feller — he's been practising here this week. Frazer, the Scottish champion.'' Then they saw Gail and Kenny walking towards them. Paul greeted them stiffly. He still hadn't forgiven Gail for her behaviour yesterday.

''Hello!'' said Kenny, anxious to make amends. ''Good luck for today — may the best man win, as they say in England.''

''The best man is you, Kenny,'' Gail put in sharply. Fortunately, they were interrupted by George bustling up.

''All right,'' he shouted. ''Let's get lined up! Frazer . . .'' His words died. Elijah was barring the way. Behind him stood a group of truculent looking hill farmers carrying a banner proclaiming. ''Get off our land.''

''What's all this?'' asked George, baffled.

''Plain enough, isn't it?'' growled Elijah, not

budging at all. "I've got twenty 'ill farmers behind me, and a writ out against you using our land. And I got the press 'ere in the meantime, so you better watch what you do!" He pointed to two earnest young men equipped with notebooks and cameras who were hastily scribbling down his every word. Gail burst into laughter.

"Well, I had always heard of these quaint old English customs, but this beats the band!"

Keeping a wary eye on Elijah and his supporters, George shepherded the competitors down to the starting line.

"All right, let's get going," he called hastily. "Pay no attention to him — we've got a contest to run."

"They'll pay attention all right before I'm through with them," muttered Elijah as they shuffled past.

The Rally continued, but the wind was proving unreliable. Duclas, the young Frenchman, came wide of the target. Lawson and McBridge overshot. One by one the competitors were eliminated, until only Paul and Kenny were left.

"Beat him, Kenny," said Gail quietly but with immense feeling. "Beat him for me."

Kenny stared at her. "You really have got it in for him, haven't you?"

She was gazing at him with frightening intensity. "Nobody speaks to me like that, Kenny, nobody."

He turned away, embarrassed and a little uneasy.

"Go!" yelled George, and Kenny lumbered forward under the weight of his kite. It was a good take off. Paul, Katie and Gail watched as he gained height. It was a splendid summer day and the huge red kite was outlined sharply against the azure sky.

Kenny dipped towards the target, making a wide sweep.

"He's running out of sky!" exclaimed Paul. "He's going to land short."

"Come on, Kenny," Gail hissed. "Find an updraught. Find one." But it was too late. He had lost too much height and landed just short of the target. The watchers on the ridge saw him struggle from his harness and begin the long climb back, carrying his kite.

"Your turn, Mr Graham!" shouted George. Paul trudged off towards his kite and then stopped aghast. His hang glider, his pride and joy, was tilted at a crazy angle with its frame twisted and the fabric ripped. Elijah was standing nearby with his cronies.

Beside himself with rage, Paul advanced on him. "What's the idea — slashing my kite?" he demanded.

"I didn't!" shouted Elijah indignantly.

"Yes you did!" Paul shouted back, almost choking with anger. "Just because I nearly hit your sheep."

"Stop it, Paul!" Katie had run up behind him and was tugging at his jacket. "Elijah, did you slash Paul's kite?"

"No, I didn't," grunted Elijah. "But I know who did." They stared at him in disbelief. "You were goin' to win today, weren't you? Even I could see that — so you had to be nobbled so you couldn't win." He stuck out a bony finger. "She did it. I saw 'er."

Gail was behind them, staring hypnotically at the ruined kite. "He's got to win!" she cried in a high unnatural voice, turning to gaze at them with wide, vacant eyes. "Why are you all staring at me like that? I had to do it, I tell you — he's got to win!" With

72

that, she turned and fled like a mad thing towards her car. She brushed past spectators and competitors and children with ice-cream cones, knocking them sideways in her haste. Before Paul and Katie could reach her, she leapt into the car and accelerated away at top speed, just as Kenny staggered up over the ridge.

"Come on!" cried Paul, dashing past him. As quick as a flash, Paul and Katie climbed into the beach buggy and the engine fired into action. Kenny dropped his kite and tumbled in after them. He did not have the faintest idea what was happening. All he knew was that for some reason they were after Gail and that she must be in terrible danger. Paul slammed his foot down and the buggy took off down the road.

Over a kilometre away by now, Gail screamed along the mountain road like one possessed. She had no idea where she was going. Indeed, she hardly knew what she was doing. Months of ever growing stress had brought her to breaking point and now it was as though something had snapped in her mind.

Gritting with concentration, Paul charged after her in the beach buggy with Kenny and Katie hanging on for dear life. The buggy may not have looked much, but it had a powerful motor and Paul was taking appalling risks, cornering almost on two wheels. But Gail, in her fast sports car, was a long way ahead and slowly edging away.

Suddenly she rounded a corner to come face to face with a flock of sheep blocking the roadway. She swerved, fighting the wheel, the brakes screeching. Then with a rending crash, the car glanced against a stone wall, bounced off and smashed into a gate. Luckily, the gate took the shock. Battered and shaken, but unhurt, Gail eased herself out of the wrecked car and started to climb towards Pikes Fell, sobbing and panting as she went.

Three minutes later the buggy arrived on the scene. "There she is!" yelled Kenny. In the distance, clambering up the rock face was Gail. They tumbled out of the buggy and raced after her.

"Gail!" screamed Kenny. "Come back! We're not going to hurt you!" But she was past listening to anyone, instead she just increased her pace, frantically seeking footholds in the shattered rock of the precipice. Paul was an experienced climber. Moving swiftly from crevice to crevice, finding cracks in the rocks which gave him purchase and always moving upwards, he quickly gained on Gail. Below him, Katie and Kenny were following as best they could. At last, Paul paused in a cleft, breathing deeply, and waited for them to reach him.

Katie looked very pale. She wedged herself as tightly as possible into the rock face next to Paul and peered out across the valley. Stone-walled fields, sheep, in the distance more mountains with cotton wool clouds drifting slowly across their peaks. She began to feel giddy and faint.

"Don't look down!" said Paul sharply. She pressed her face against the cool rock, sweating. Now Kenny had caught them up.

"Not used to this sort of thing," he muttered apologetically. "Where's . . ." There was an ominous crack. Gail in her hurry had dislodged a boulder and it now came thumping down the face towards them. As it fell, it brought down a rain of surface rock and stone.

"Look out!" yelled Paul, throwing himself against the rock face. It was not a moment too soon — an avalanche of stones and rocks came hurtling down towards them. With a deafening rumble, the boulder shot over their heads, splintering into fragments as it hit the solid ledge below. Dust rose in clouds and the very cliff face shook as rock after rock came crashing down at them before bounding into the abyss below.

At last the frightful bombardment stopped, the last stones trickled and pattered over them. Gail had made a convulsive movement to save herself when the boulder had broken away beneath her feet, and she had managed to roll into a cleft in the rocks.

"Stay here," said Paul, and began to climb towards her. Kenny looked at Katie. She was covered with dust, just as he was, and there was a cut on her forehead.

"You O.K.?" he whispered, afraid that if he raised his voice he might bring another avalanche of stones down on them.

"I'm fine," said Katie, attempting to smile. They looked upwards. Far above them, Paul had reached Gail. She was the colour of the rocks against which she was lying, and there were tears of frustration and anger on her face.

"I've hurt my leg," she gasped as Paul pulled himself into the cleft. "I can't move." Paul had taken a course with Mountain Rescue and knew how to deal with such cases. He grasped her ankle tenderly and tried to rotate it. She gave a gasp of pain.

"Don't move," said Paul. He felt a stab of anxiety. Here, stranded high up on the cliff face, it would be hours before anything could be done, and Gail was suffering from acute shock. That was obvious. Suddenly, inspiration came to him. He waved to Katie and Kenny, two minute faces far below. Katie saw him.

"They can't move!" she exclaimed. "Gail must be hurt." Paul was making a circular movement with

his hand.

"What does he mean?" asked Kenny, bewildered.

"I know," said Katie suddenly. She began scrambling down the rocks.

Going down a cliff is far worse then going up. She often had to cling to a ledge, swearing under her breath while her feet sought a foothold. Twice she slid helplessly down loose stone screes to fetch up with a bump on the rocks further down. At last, dusty, bruised and aching in every limb, she managed to reach the buggy and snatched up the walkie talkie.

"Colin — Colin!" she called breathlessly. "We've got trouble — on Pikes Fell!" As luck had it, Colin and Nigel were out on a routine patrol when Katie's call came through. Colin turned his helicopter and flew towards Pikes Fell.

While Katie was summoning their rescue, Paul had taken his jacket off and tucked it round Gail. She was as white as a sheet and her teeth were chattering, but she was quiet now, as though a storm had blown out in her mind leaving her perfectly calm but exhausted.

"I suppose I've been very stupid," she said, forcing a weak smile.

"You have rather," Paul agreed. "But don't worry about it. It was you, wasn't it, that ripped up my kite?".

"I just couldn't bear the thought of your winning. I'll pay for the kite." Paul nodded painfully. There didn't seem to be anything he could say.

Up above, Colin was seeking them. But Pikes Fell was an enormous place — an army could easily have hidden in its forbidding cliffs. He turned the helicopter for another sweep, gazing intently at the mountain landscape as it flew rapidly past. Then he noticed two tiny figures in bright anoraks.

"O.K. Nigel," he said crisply. "Stand by with the hoist."

Paul held on to Gail as the chopper came in, its blast almost knocking them from the ledge. The hoist swung down to them.

"Don't be afraid," said Paul, fixing it securely round her. "They know what they are doing." He steadied her as the winch lifted, then she was away, swinging gently like a pendulum. She waved to Paul as Nigel helped her through the hatch and then the helicopter rose and turned for base.

****

Dawn had just broken across the mountains as David finished his long drive from London. He decided to look in at Scarsdale on the off chance that someone might be up to make him some coffee. As it was both Katie and Margaret had risen early — Katie had been unable to get to sleep properly after all yesterday's excitement and her moving around downstairs had woken Margaret too. They told him about the adventure on Pikes Fell, Paul's ripped kite, the dreadful climb and the helicopter rescue while they bustled about him making breakfast.

So it was a very thoughtful man who turned into the yard at Grimsdyke later that morning. He had wondered once or twice if Paul had it in him to make a good Park Ranger. Oh, he was keen enough, and he had courage — that business with the rabid dog had proved that. But he was very young — did he have the judgement and clear headed care one needed in the job? Now he had few doubts on the subject.

Paul was stretched out on the settee, poring through a local guide book when David came in.

"Had a good trip?" he asked casually.

"Not bad," said David, flinging off his jacket. "I hear you've been having some excitement up here."

"A bit," said Paul. He looked carefully up at David. "Oh, there's a letter for you — from Elijah, I think it is."

David ripped it open while Paul watched anxiously. "Well this is a bit thick!" he exclaimed after a brief perusal of the contents. "It's Elijah's damn writ against hang-gliding. We can fight it, of course."

"What do you think the chances are?"

"For hang-gliding? Oh about evens. Still, if the worse comes to the worse and they throw you out, you can always take up another hobby." He laughed. "Psychiatry, perhaps?"

CHAPTER FOUR

TREASURE!

A week later, the weather changed suddenly. It was now blowing hard and huge black thunder clouds were piling up over the peaks. An old jeep creaked up the mountain road towards Eskdale. It's driver was a stocky man in his thirties with a somewhat stupid expression. Next to him sat a tall man, a little older than his companion, gripping a dog-eared map. In the back, partly hidden by a worn tarpaulin that flapped heavily in the wind, was a stack of what appeared to be mining gear — drills, picks and shovels, a geiger counter, and some cases marked *'Danger - Explosives.'*

The driver brought the jeep to a grinding halt by a signpost.

"How's that for map reading, Derek?" said his companion. "Bearsdale National Park — right on the nail!"

"I still don't see why we got to go and see him, Vic," Derek grumbled.

"He could ask awkward questions, rumble us!"

Vic laughed quietly. He had a peculiar way of laughing without any particular reason that was not very pleasant. "He'll ask awkward questions if he finds us snooping around his Park and we haven't told him we're here." His voice took on a rougher edge. "Now get on with it. We haven't got all the time in the world."

At Grimsdyke, Paul and David were poring over a large map spread out between them.

"Bearsdale Trackway," David announced. "I've been working on the idea for months. A route for people on foot and horseback, following the highest ridges, more than sixty kilometres long. Camping places, under strict conditions, so as not to spoil the landscape, here and — here. Signposted fords marked, gates set up through the stone walls." He paused for breath. "It would cost, but I've had a word with the County Council and I think I can get them to cough up a grant. The whole point would be to give people from the big cities just south of here a chance to enjoy a magnificent countryside without ruining it. But you know what hill farmers are — they're an independent lot. I'll have to go down on my knees to them, I expect. You'll have to, too!"

At that moment, there was a sharp knock on the door. Paul opened it, and saw two men standing there. The taller man was smiling in a friendly way, but his companion seemed rather ill at ease.

"Sorry to disturb you," said the tall man, still smiling. "I'm Vic Johns — and this is Derek Howell — you were expecting us at eleven, I think."

"Right!" said David, rising and putting the map away. "I'm David Martin, Park Warden, and this is Paul Graham. Welcome to Bearsdale."

"Thanks," said Vic. "Well, as I told you, we're from the Cambridge Ecology Unit. We're doing a survey on wild birds."

Paul cut in; he had been a keen bird-watcher at school. "Any particular species?"

The two men exchanged glances. "Er, no," said Vic. "We're casting our net very wide."

"Yeah, very wide," added Derek, helplessly. The conversation dropped.

"Well, how can we help you?" David said at last as nobody else was going to say anything.

"Common courtesy, Mr Martin!" said Vic. "We'll be prowling about in the Park so we thought we would just drop in to say hello and what we're here for, and then if anyone reports two strangers, you'll know it's us."

"Fine," said David, rather baffled. "Well, if there's anything we can do, just get in touch with us. Where are you staying?"

"We're not fixed up yet," said Vic.

Paul butted in again. "Try the Jacksons — first turning on the left past the village and up the lane on the right. Tell them Paul sent you."

"Thanks we will," said Vic, and Derek nodded his agreement. Paul showed them out.

"Nice fellas," he said, coming back. David nodded and started to unfold the map again.

"Wild birds. Whatever will they think of next."

Outside, Vic and Derek climbed into their jeep and drove off. "See?" said Vic. "We can do whatever we like now. No questions asked."

"Yeah, that young one's got enough questions for two."

"Natural curiosity at his age," Vic breezed, airily. "You worry too much, that's your trouble."

Before long, they drew up outside Scarsdale Farm. "This looks like the place," said Derek.

"A Vet's! No thanks!" Vic retorted. "Too many comings and goings for my liking." As they were backing out, Katie appeared on horseback.

"Morning!" she greeted them cheerfully.

"Morning," mumbled Derek.

"Lost your way?"

"Yes, but we're O.K. now," said Vic hastily before Derek could put his foot in it. "Sorry!"

The next moment the jeep was gone. Katie rode Nero into the yard, dismounted, and started to unsaddle him without giving the two men another thought.

They had gone a kilometre from Scarsdale when their jeep was held up on the road by a large flock of sheep. Derek was no countryman and made the mistake of trying to force his way through. The flock panicked immediately, lambs crying out for ewes, and ewes frantically running up and down the narrow lane. In the midst of this commotion, a furious old man appeared, waving his stick at the two men.

"What the 'eck do think you're up to, you stupid road 'ogs!" Elijah raged. "I've taken your number, oh yes — and I'm going to tell the police!"

"Very sorry sir," said Vic in what he thought was his most placating manner. "We're strangers here — didn't realise how narrow the lanes are. Won't happen again, I promise you."

"No, it ruddy well won't!" stormed the old man, brandishing his stick just under Derek's nose. "If you touch just one, just one, you'll pay for it — full market price!"

"Sorry." Then Vic had a better thought. "Here, this fiver will cover any damage, I hope. No need to involve the police, is there. I mean we haven't done any harm."

"'Arm!" sniffed the old man, pocketing the money with surprising speed. "I don't know. City folk, dashin' about." He stumped off towards a dilapidated hill farm set back from the road, whistling to Timber as he went. The sheep trotted obediently before them. Vic breathed a sigh of relief.

"Let's move on," said Derek, but Vic was looking at Elijah's farm with great interest.

"This will do us. Nothing around here, no callers from one month to the next. Made for the job!"

"It's a dump," Derek muttered gloomily.

"Sure it is," replied Vic. "Couldn't be better. Drive in, but mind his blasted sheep this time."

Elijah was about to close the gate as they pulled in. "What do you want now?" he asked crossly.

"Who owns this place?" said Vic, ignoring the old man's unsociable tone.

"I do, of course — can't afford no grand farm 'ands these days."

"Can you put us up? We want somewhere quiet, where we won't be disturbed." Vic waved a ten pound note in Elijah's face. He snatched it, sniffed it and then looked up at them through his bushy eyebrows.

"I can only spare one room — and it's not up to much."

"We're not fussy."

"Better not be," Elijah retorted, leading the way to his farmhouse. Derek was left to carry the luggage.

Vic almost baulked at the sight of Elijah's kitchen. There was a friendly enough log fire burning in the grate, but above the fire was a blackened picture of the Kaiser, looking extremely fierce, and on another wall an ancient poster of Kitchener, looking even fiercer and saying *'Your Country needs You!'* On the table was a dirty old teapot, a tea caddy marked *'A present from Margate'* and a few tattered books, *'Tales from the Crypt'* and *'Tombstone Stories'* being among them. Elijah liked a good read in the evenings before going to bed.

Timber rolled over by the fire and began to scratch busily at fleas.

"What do you want up here anyway?" asked Elijah. He sounded quite resentful despite the fact that he had pocketed the ten pound note with alacrity. "What's wrong with the village pub, or Jackson's place, come to that?"

"I told you, we want somewhere quiet," said Vic, patiently. "I can see you don't like strangers, nor do we — and we want to concentrate on our work."

"What work's that then?" Elijah asked suspiciously.

"We're making a survey of wild birds," explained Vic.

"For Cambridge University," added Derek, who up to that moment had stood there speechless at the sight of their lodgings.

"Too much of that goin' on these days," muttered Elijah darkly. "When I was a lad there were none of it, none. I'll get some blankets," and he left the room.

Derek whistled, "Talk about living rough." He sat down carefully on the end of a lumpy sofa. His comment met with no reply. Vic was already looking at the map he had been following.

"It will do," he said absentmindedly. "Now we're here — and here's the quarry we're after!" Derek looked over his shoulder.

"That's close," he said with what for him passed as cheerfulness. "Great!"

****

Thornby Quarry lay high on the flanks of Eskdale Crag, at the end of a long winding track. All around was desolation — bare rocks, dry heather and high mountain pasture, fit for little but the toughest mountain sheep. The quarry itself had been abandoned many years ago. Huge shattered blocks of granite lay everywhere.

The day that had promised so much rain had now given way to brilliant sunshine, a lark was singing as Vic and Derek arrived in their jeep, but they did not recognise it.

"Is this it?" exclaimed Derek, incredulously. "Doesn't look as if there's been gold here to me."

"How do you know what a disused gold mine looks like?" demanded Vic. "I checked it out, don't forget, and where there's gold, there's uranium. Come on, and bring all that gear." He strode down into the quarry and Derek trudged after him, bent under three large boxes of dynamite and the prospecting gear.

Arriving at the quarry floor, Vic sat down on his haunches and started to move the Geiger counter across the rock. It registered nothing and he moved on, sweeping it slowly from side to side. After almost an hour of this he sat back to rest on the loose surface.

"This is great!" grumbled Derek, sitting in the dust beside him, and mopping at his brow with his shirt sleeve. "About enough uranium here to drive a rubber duck across a bath!"

"Better try the seismic method," said Vic, thoughtfully.

"Seismic — what's that?"

"You bore holes in the rock," explained Vic as patiently as possible, "then you put charges of dynamite down them and set them off. The shock registers on this thing here. It's called seismic surveying."

"What's that then?"

"I've read it all up," said Vic. He saw that Derek was impressed and warmed to his subject. "From the readings on this thing, you can build up a picture of the rock formation beneath. That way, we can tell where the uranium is, see? Now let's get started shall we?"

Not far away, Paul was driving his beach buggy towards Pikes Fell. He was in the highest of spirits, for David had given him his first really responsible job. He was to work out the first five or six kilometres of Bearsdale Trackway. Using the large scale map that David had drawn, he was to mark out the exact route, look over the fords, and talk to the hill farmers along the proposed way.

He pushed the buggy rather fast through the first ford he came to, raising clouds of spray. Then charging up the steep track that led out of it, he stopped at the top of the ridge, took out the map, and spread it out before him so as to have a good look. He was so absorbed that he did not notice Elijah approach.

"What are you doin' on my land?" he bellowed in Paul's ear. "Get off it! Go on, before I set my dog on yer."

"I'm sorry," said Paul, startled by this sudden attack. "I was just working out something. I didn't know I was on your land here."

"Ah, well you are," said Elijah. "And what are you workin' out? Let me see." He grabbed the map out of Paul's hands and glared at it. "What's this!" He stabbed the thin red line that meandered across the Park.

"It's the new trackway, we're planning," said Paul. He had a feeling that Elijah would not be very sympathetic to the cause, but decided to have a shot at convincing him anyway. "You see, we think hikers and people on holiday..."

"'Ikers!" exploded Elijah. "I don't 'old with them — don't 'old with city folk. I'm not 'avin' a trackway across my land! You can tell your boss so."

"I'm sure we can come to some arrangement," said Paul hastily. Elijah seemed to be groping for words. Bristling with rage, he raised his stick at Paul, who retreated quickly behind his vehicle.

"Get out!" gasped Elijah, finding his voice at last. "Go on!" Paul drove off in haste. The other people he saw were less obstinate and that afternoon, his work completed for the day, Paul turned in at Scarsdale.

Margaret was just finishing surgery when Paul looked in. An immense tom cat sat glowering on the surgery table, held securely by an extremely small girl.

"Keep him still, Rosemary," said Margaret, examining his hind leg. "Has he been fighting?"

"No," Rosemary declared firmly. "He never fights."

"He goes out at night, doesn't he?" The little girl nodded. "Then how do you know he doesn't fight?" said Margaret smiling at her.

"He's too nice to fight."

Margaret started to prepare the big tom for his injection. "Wouldn't he fight if he was in danger?"

"Don't know," said Rosemary and bit her lip.

Margaret filled a hypodermic and Rosemary covered her face with her hands

At the Quarry, Vic was inserting a stick of dynamite with extreme care down the hole that Derek had bored. He connected the fuse with an electrical detonator and looked at Derek who was blocking his ears and screwing up his eyes. "There's no need to do that yet," he said coldly. "I haven't finished yet."

In the surgery, Rosemary was still standing with her hands over her eyes while Margaret cleaned up the tom's wounds. "You can look now, it's all over," she smiled. "Bring him back in a couple of days, and I'll have a look at him."

"Thank you," said Rosemary, stowing the tom into his basket. "How much is it please?"

"I'll put it on your father's account," said Margaret. The little girl left murmuring her thanks.

"How long does it take to learn to be a vet?" asked Paul who had been watching.

"I'm still learning!" laughed Margaret, washing her hands.

"No, I mean to qualify?"

"Oh, several years. Thinking of taking it up?"

"No, I just wondered," said Paul. "It must be great, doing all that for animals. Being a Park

Warden means so much paper work.''

"So does being a vet!'' she retorted, laughing.

"Where's Katie?'' asked Paul. "Out riding?'' Margaret nodded, absorbed in cleaning up the surgery table. "I've got the day off, do you think I might take Lady and catch her up?''

"Of course, How's your riding getting on by the way? Katie says...'' The air was suddenly split by a loud muffled boom, like the sound of distant artillery. "What was that!'' she said, startled.

"I don't know,'' said Paul. "Sounded like an explosion.'' Again, the thudding boom filled the air like far off thunder. But the day had cleared and there was no cloud. Paul stared at Margaret without a word and Margaret stared back at him.

They were not the only people, puzzled by the strange sound. David was out mending a gate, driving the post in with massive blows from his weighty sledge hammer when he heard the first boom. He paused in his work, listening. The sound came again, echoing round the valley. Katie heard it too as she cantered across Eskdale Moor, and Elijah as he shepherded his ewes to another pasture. Not one of them could imagine where the sound came from, or what it could mean.

Vic was in the process of inserting another charge of dynamite into the ground. He connected it with the detonator and Derek blocked his ears again and winced. "Ruddy coward, you are,'' he said, and pressed the plunger. There was a huge muffled boom, and the ground shook beneath them.

"How much longer do we have to go on doing this?'' Derek whined plaintively.

"Until we find what we're looking for,'' replied Vic, noting the reading. "Get on with it. We haven't got all day.''

Katie was trotting sedately on the crest of the great ridge above Eskdale when Paul caught up with her.

"You really are improving," laughed Katie as he galloped up. "I think I'll let you have another go on Nero next week...." A loud boom flooded the valley and the horses lunged nervously.

"Steady, boy — steady," said Katie, patting Nero's neck. "It's alright! Steady — good boy." Paul gazed down the valley, but he could not make out the direction of the sound.

"I've heard that noise twice today. They're not thunder, and they're not sonic booms — they don't come from up there," he pointed upwards with his free hand, but Katie was not looking. Her eyes were fixed on the mountain ranges towards Thornby.

"Seems to come from that direction," she said, frowning. They turned their horses towards Thornby and rode hard for twenty minutes. Then they stopped to listen beside a wide stream. Silence but for the gentle sound of trickling water.

"Oh come on!" said Paul. "Let's leave it! You're coming to dinner tonight — and I'm cooking!" Katie gave a dreadful groan and he chased her, laughing, down the hill slope.

Meanwhile, Vic and Derek had given up for the day and were trudging back to their jeep.

"Dead loss," muttered Derek, sweating under his load of gear.

"Give it a chance!" Vic shouted, striding ahead of him. "We've only been at it one day — we haven't even covered a tenth of the ground yet."

"No wonder you didn't qualify," said Derek, pausing for breath. He shifted the weight of the gear and staggered on.

"What do you mean?" asked Vic. There was an

ominous edge to his voice.

"As a geologist. Oh yes, you've read all the books! You said that when you went for that job with the New South Wales Government, and look what came of that! Then you say you've found a map of a quarry in Bearsdale!" The two men bickered all the way to the jeep, and all the way back to Elijah's farm. When they arrived however, they had to stop quarrelling like it or not. They were determined not to let Elijah in on their secret. Instead they maintained a stony silence while Elijah served them lamb chops, badly burned from a greasy frying pan, underdone boiled potatoes with the skins still hanging from them, and thick wedges of plain, unbuttered bread. Elijah was not a man of many words. When they had finished, he settled down by the fire with *'Tales from the Crypt,'* while Vic and Derek stared gloomily into the burning logs and wondered what tomorrow would bring.

Over at Grimsdyke, they were eating in better style. Paul had become so sick of their endless diet of bacon and eggs that he had bought a cook book and started to make experiments of his own. David had been treated to roast beef, and steak and kidney pie, and even pizza. There had been failures, as when Paul had proudly produced an apple pie that managed to be thoroughly burnt on top and equally thoroughly underdone underneath. But Paul had improved steadily and now he was sniffing at an enormous hot pot, stirring and tasting and adding things from the spice box. An effort had been made to tidy things up. Socks and shirts had been crammed into a cupboard and a cloth laid over the table. There were even candles stuck into bottles, as well as wine.

"At least the wine will be drinkable," said David, getting out a corkscrew. Katie hovered close to Paul criticising his efforts.

"Isn't the gas a bit high?" she suggested. She too fancied herself as a cook.

"No, it isn't too high," said Paul crossly.

"Well, can I help?"

"No!"

"But Paul..."

Margaret burst out laughing, "Oh, for heavens sake sit down, Katie. It's their party — just leave them to it!"

David poured the wine. "I heard the strangest noise while I was out today," he remarked, "like distant guns."

"We heard it too!" exclaimed Katie. "What do you think it is?"

"I don't know," said David thoughtfully, looking at the map on the wall. "But it might help if we knew where it was coming from. Have you any ideas?"

"I thought it came from about here," Katie went over and pointed.

"Thornby Quarry!" exclaimed David. "Are you sure?"

"No," she admitted. "I'm not certain, but I think so. Paul was with me — he thought so too."

David stared at the map, lost in thought.

"Blasting?" suggested Margaret. "They do blasting in quarries after all."

David shook his head. He left the map and drew his chair up to the table. "The place hasn't been used for years. It wasn't really a quarry anyway. It was a mine. Open cast mining they used to call it — for gold."

"Gold!" squealed Katie, excited. "Maybe there's still gold there! Maybe..."

"Yes, maybe," said David. "Why don't you

and Paul have a look tomorrow? I would like to know what's going on."

Paul arrived with the hot pot. Boeuf Carbonnade!" he announced grandly.

"Oh — casserole," said Katie.

"Not at all," said Paul, hurt by her derision of this, his greatest culinary effort to date. David tasted it and exchanged glances with Margaret.

"Excellent!" he said with an effort. "Really good, isn't it, Margaret?"

****

Elijah was chopping logs at the back of his cottage. As he swung his axe, he heard voices raised in anger coming from the kitchen. He was a nosy old man, and he was already wondering just what his lodgers were really up to, so he put down his axe, crept up to the kitchen window and listened intently.

"Pack it in!" he heard Vic shout furiously. "I've just about had enough of you!"

"You won't listen to anything I say, will you?" complained Derek. "You treat me like some sort of stooge." Vic jumped towards Derek and lifted his fist to his face.

"I'll treat you as I ruddy like, and you'll do as you're told. Do you understand me?"

For once, Derek stood his ground. "Oh yeah, I understand you very well, It's just that I'm getting tired of all your high flown ideas, all the big plans that don't come to nothing! I'm tired of going to that ruddy quarry."

Vic banged the table with rage, luckily it was sturdier than it seemed. "O.K. If you don't like it, shove off. I don't need you! I can manage very well by myself mate. So shove off!"

Suddenly Derek lost his nerve. He was not very bright, and he had followed Vic faithfully through a whole series of rather dubious adventures, at home and abroad. Though most of them had ended in utter disaster, he would be lost without Vic. "Don't be like that, Vic," he whined placatingly. "I'm just as keen as you are to find this ruddy uranium! Don't get me wrong."

"Then go find your own. See if you can find any without maps or gear. Then I won't have to share the loot will I?"

Drooping visibly, Derek sat down on the table.

"Come on Vic, I didn't mean it like that. We've always been mates, haven't we? Let's work together like we always have — equal partners?" Vic looked sharply at him. He needed Derek almost as much as Derek needed him. He decided to take a different tack.

"O.K." he said churlishly. "But if you step out of line again, I'll do you. Understand?"

"Yeah," said Derek gratefully. "Look how do we get the stuff out when we find it? It's got to be refined hasn't it?"

"I got pals in the mining business," said Vic. "We'll set up a company, get permission to mine here. Course, we'll tie up the royalties first — and we won't say it's uranium. We'll say it's building stone or something like that. That ought to keep them quiet."

"Building stone!" chortled Derek. "I like that. That will really fox them. Won't it? Building stone — that's really great!"

"Let's get on with it, then," said Vic, and they left the house. Elijah was chopping wood again as they came out.

"Ey!" he called. "Was it you makin' those

bangs yesterday?"

"Bangs, what bangs?" asked Derek, stopping short.

Vic cut in smoothly, "Those bangs we heard. You remember. When we were by that stream watching those wagtails."

"What? Oh yeah, wagtails," Derek agreed, confused.

"Probably planes going through the sound barrier," said Vic. "R.A.F. exercises — could go on for a day or two."

Elijah peered keenly up at them. "Funny, it started just when you two turned up."

"You suggesting something?"

"All I'm sayin' is that it's funny," said Elijah stubbornly.

"Yeah, coincidences can be. Very funny," said Vic. "Come on Derek, we've got work to do."

Elijah watched them go, axe in hand. His expression was one of extreme cunning mixed with caution. He put down the axe, picked up his stout stick and strode off purposefully in the direction of the Quarry.

Vic and Derek climbed out of their jeep and went down into the Quarry. Vic was only carrying the map, but Derek was as usual encumbered by picks and shovels, boxes of dynamite and gear of every conceivable type. When they reached the spot they had been investigating the day before, Derek dumped the gear with a huge sigh and they started work. Little did they know that Elijah was stumping towards them across the wastes of Eskdale, and neither of them knew that Paul and Katie were also on their way.

Katie pulled Nero in and listened, her head cocked on one side. There was nothing to be heard but the sigh of wind across the heather. They rode on for only a couple of minutes when there was a sudden distant boom.

"It's Thornby all right!" said Katie. They quickened their pace towards the Quarry, not knowing what to expect.

Down in the Quarry, Derek was grumbling miserably. The sun was high and the dust thick and he was very thirsty.

"Keep at it," said Vic curtly. They started to lay another charge, unaware that Elijah had found their jeep parked on the edge of the Quarry and was, even now, gazing down at them. He watched Derek lay the charge and nearly jumped out of his skin when the loud boom erupted. Gripping his stick firmly, he clambered down towards them, through the tumbled rocks. Vic was in the process of connecting another set of fuses when a voice broke his concentration.

"Funny bird-watchin' isn't it?" There was Elijah, standing at the bottom of the Quarry, looking at them.

"Hello," said Vic, coolly. "What are you doing here?"

"I'm no fool," Elijah said. "I know what yer doin' 'ere."

"Do you?" said Vic. "Then go away."

"Lot of money in uranium isn't there?" Vic and Derek exchanged alarmed glances. "Don't worry," hissed Elijah, with infinite cunning. "I won't tell. I won't breathe a word to anyone. Let's just agree that I say nothin' about it, and you give me a cut on the uranium when you find it."

Vic chuckled heartily. "So that's it! You get a share in our treasure. That's all you want!"

"Aye, that's it," said Elijah, pleased that things were going so smoothly. Vic laughed uproariously, and Elijah joined in, but the laughter died on his lips when he saw Vic produce a pistol and point it at him.

Paul and Katie were galloping up the ridge towards the Quarry. As they mounted the crest of the ridge above it, they saw an open jeep round the corner at top speed and charge furiously down the steep track. In it were three people, one driving, another struggling furiously in the grip of a tall man in the back.

"It's Elijah!" yelled Katie. She wheeled Nero round in a flash and took off after them, Paul following hard on her heels. There would have been no chance of catching up with Vic's jeep had Katie not known Beasrsdale so well, but she knew that there was no turning off the lane down which the jeep was heading for more than a kilometre.

"Come on!" she cried. "We'll cut them off!" She turned Nero, urging him into a full gallop and took him across the nearest stone wall. Paul had no choice but to go after her. Lady flew over the wall like a bird. He lost a stirrup as they landed and grabbed at the saddle, but somehow he stayed with Lady, found the stirrup and went on after Katie. They dashed through a shallow stream, splashing Paul with mud from head to foot, and on up a narrow track through the heather. Slowly he gained on Katie until he finally caught up with Nero and they rushed on together, neck and neck.

****

Biting his lower lip with concentration, Derek drove the jeep at top speed down the rutted lane. Elijah was an elderly man, but he had spent his whole life in the open and was built like a steel spring. Twice he almost managed to knock Vic out of the back of the jeep as it crashed and jolted down the lane.

"What are we going to do with him?" yelled Derek, fighting the wheel as they hit a large pothole in the road.

"Get rid of him, of course, you numbskull!" Vic cried, dodging a heavy blow from Elijah.

"How?"

"I don't know!" he shouted, holding on with one hand and fighting off Elijah with the other. "I'm trying to think!"

As the two riders chased down a gravelly bank leading to the lane, Katie suddenly pointed and shouted. "There they are!"

The jeep was coming towards them, up hill now, along the lane that zig-zagged from the Quarry. Derek saw the two youngsters and yelled a warning but Vic had already spotted them. With his captor's attention drawn, Elijah grabbed his chance. He struck Vic's pistol hand down against the tailboard of the jeep. The gun flew out of Vic's hand onto the road, and Vic was flung backwards against Derek who lost control. There was a loud grinding as Derek stamped frantically on the brakes, and the squeal of tortured rubber as the tyres lost their grip. Spinning round, the jeep hit the stone wall with a dreadful crash and turned over onto its side, catapulting the three men into the road. The blow knocked Derek and Elijah unconscious but Vic reeled to his feet to see Paul and Katie bearing down on him. Hardly knowing what he was doing, he seized a big slab of stone from the wall, and swung it at Katie. Nero bolted and Lady shied violently, throwing Paul to the ground.

Vic shouted something, but lying flat on his back, dazed and breathless, Paul could not take it in. As though in a dream, he watched Vic lift the great stone and swing it down with all his might. He had

just enough wits left to roll aside before the stone
cracked against the wall next to him.

Gasping with shock and rage, Vic lifted and
swung the big slab again. Then, all of a sudden, a

look of surprise came over his face. The stone slipped
from his hands and he crumpled into the road.
Standing where Vic had been was Elijah, his stout
stick in hand.

"Tit for tat, that is," he grunted complacently,
tapping the stick in his hand.

****

Margaret had asked Paul and David to dinner, and
Katie was determined to outdo Paul at cooking. She
was toiling busily over the stove when they arrived.
Margaret poured wine for their visitors at the table.

"Well come on!" she said. "Was it uranium they were after, or not?"

David laughed. "Yes it was! The funny thing is, they're not even proper geologists — when they didn't get anything on their geiger counter they tried using seismic readings." This met with a gale of laughter from Paul.

"That's no way to find uranium! Even I know that!"

"Well," David went on, grinning, "Vic had been reading some book."

"What made them pick on that Quarry of all places?" asked Margaret.

David took a sip of wine before replying. "There used to be gold there — and where there was gold there could be uranium. Thank goodness there isn't any or we'd have a uranium rush on our hands. Anyway, we won't be seeing much more of our budding prospectors — there's a list of charges as long as my arm against them at the station."

Katie arrived with a magnificent golden souffle on a silver tray. "Hey presto!" she cried, setting it down in the centre of the table. There followed a deep sighing noise and with a gurgle, the great souffle subsided into a gooey mass. Everyone burst out laughing. In fact, Margaret became so helpless that David had to thump her firmly on the back and Paul could hardly see through tears of laughter.

"Oh well," he gasped. "After last night, we're just about evens!" Somewhat nettled, Katie tipped what was left of the souffle over his head. He stopped laughing abruptly and everyone stared at him as the sticky yellow sludge oozed over his face. Then everybody simply roared with laughter — in fact they went on laughing right through their dinner. A good plate of bacon and eggs!

CHAPTER FIVE

WASTE

Clouds of dust enveloped David as he drove his battered landrover through Eskdale forest. Autumn was fast approaching and the trees were turning a warm golden brown. All around the air was full of the noise of power saws and now and then came a loud whistling noise — the sound of air rushing through the branches of a falling tree, followed by a muffled thump as it hit the ground. A tractor rumbled across his path, dragging a bundle of cut logs.

The road petered out before a hugh paper mill on the edge of a rushing stream, framed by the grey mountains that towered over it. David stopped the landrover and jumped out. A big man in his forties, clad in check shirt and jeans and wearing a bright red helmet, was directing the work. At the sight of David, he turned, a broad grin creasing his sun-burned face and sending tiny wrinkles chasing round his eyes.

"Almost went into you, that tractor did," he observed with a nod of his head. He had a marked Canadian accent.

David did not waste words, "Tom Barry?"
"Yep."

"I'm David Martin, Park Warden. Can I have a word with you?"

The big man pushed his helmet back from his sweating brow. "Sure. Come into my office — can't hear myself speak!"

A few moments later, they were in the wooden hut that served Tom as an office. Pinned on the walls were maps of the forest. A bright modern stove filled one corner with a coffee percolator bubbling on it, and in the middle of the room was a large solid oak desk heaped with tottering piles of papers.

"Coffee?" asked Tom. "I always keep a pot going."

David sat on the only clear edge of the desk. "Thanks," he said. "Hot isn't it? You wouldn't believe how cold it can be here in winter."

"Not as cold as Canada," replied Tom, pouring coffee into two battered tin mugs. "How long have you been here?"

"Almost three years now. I feel as if I was born in the place." Tom chucked a bag of sugar lumps in David's direction. "How are you settling down?"

"O.K." Tom drawled. "Of course, I've only been here a few months." David sipped his coffee. It was strong, coal-black and very hot. Fortunately that was the way he liked it.

"Tom, I'm responsible among other things for the ecology here." Tom looked puzzled. "The balance of nature. Left to itself, nature usually keeps things steady. In Canada, for example, wolves prey on the Caribou herds." Tom stirred his mug with a pencil — he seemed short of spoons.

"Sure," he remarked. "If they didn't the Caribou would increase to the point where they starved. Also the wolves take the weakest."

"Exactly! It's just like that here," explained

David "The streams here are full of trout. There are deer on the high grounds and all sorts of wild life. They all stay roughly in balance, unless man interferes."

"Like hunters and tourists?" put in Tom.

"And industry." Tom looked at him sharply, and David went on, "I know there's got to be industry Tom. We want people to stay here and not have to go to the towns. But we've got to make sure that it doesn't tilt the balance of nature."

"You think that we do?"

David sighed and put his mug down on the desk. "You've got a gang of young chaps down at the paper mill. Contract workers aren't they?" He received a brief nod from Tom. "Well, I've had some complaints. They've been charging about on their motor bikes, scaring the sheep, disturbing the wild life. I've checked and it's got to stop."

After a pause Tom spoke. "I'll see to it. Was there anything else?"

David laughed, "Just one thing. You're staying with the Barton's aren't you. Do they feed you well?"

His question was received with raised eyebrows and a chuckle. "So, so. I get a bit tired of bacon and eggs!"

"Come to supper tonight then," David said. "My assistant, Paul, is doing the cooking. He's promised to make something good!"

While they were chatting, Katie was exercising Nero on the headland above Eskdale forest. The ground was hard after the prolonged summer drought, and she had taken him gently across the mountain tracks. But here, on the heather, she could let him have full rein. The wind whistled in her ears as she put him into a furious gallop; the big chestnut surging eagerly forward under her at the merest touch of her heels.

Far away, the mountains of the border rose purplish in the distant haze. Exhilarated by the beauty around her and the lightning speed of her mount, Katie took Nero across a rushing stream and a loose stone wall in swift succession. Then, as he began to breathe deeply, she pulled him in from their long gallop and they trotted up to a man in a tweed suit sitting on a rough pile of loose stones.

"Mr. Rowse!" she exclaimed. "Haven't you got a class today? I thought the village school started term this week. I don't have to be back until next week, thank goodness!" Her chatter met with no reply from Rowse. He seemed not to hear her. His gaze was fixed on something in the valley below. Then he turned his craggy face to her.

"There's an outbreak of flu in the village." He seemed to talk to himself rather than her. "As you know, I have only twenty pupils. Since nine of them failed to turn up today, I gave the rest of them the day off."

Katie sat down on the rocks next to him companionably. "I see! Won't you be in trouble?"

Vacantly, Rowse lit his pipe before replying. "The people round here are noted for their rugged independence. Have you not noticed that?"

She laughed. "Yes, I have. In fact I noticed the moment....."

Rowse suddenly gripped her arm. "Look!" he whispered, pointing. She followed his gaze. High above them, silhouetted against the clear sky, wheeled a mountain eagle. They watched it in silence

104

for some minutes before Rowse spoke again.

"Fine creature, isn't it? It's a pity they are dying out!" Katie gave him a look of surprise and Rowse nodded grimly. "Oh yes they are. Do you know why?" As Katie saw that he was going to tell her whether she replied or not, she remained silent. "Look that way, Miss Jackson," Rowse commanded, pointing a bony finger. She looked obediently. At the bottom of the valley stood a vast concrete complex — a giant dome, cooling towers, a maze of piping and what looked like a control centre or office block.

"It's been going up for years."

Rowse removed the pipe from his mouth and jabbed the stem at her. "Quite so. Scoresby Nuclear Power. It started up last week, I am told. Spilling out poison!" Katie was startled by the expression of pure hate on his face as he continued. "I've spoken to the County Council. I've collected a petition from every man in these parts to send to Parliament, but they won't listen."

She cut in, "Mr Rowse, you can't put the clock back. We need power — and that place is built now, and working. They've spent eight million pounds..."

"So I am told. Well it may have started operations but it doesn't mean they have to go on. I'm going to see to that!"

Rowse seemed lost in his thoughts once more. His eyes were fixed, full of implacable hatred on the big complex down in the valley. Watching him with concern, Katie sought for words and could find none. He kept staring into the valley, his chin resting on his gnarled hands and his hands on his walking stick. He did not even seem to notice when Katie mounted Nero and rode off. He did not even say goodbye.

That evening, David gave dinner to Tom, as he had promised. Paul was busy at the stove, stirring a large pot from which came rich comfortable bubblings and a wonderful scent of hot spicy beef. Margaret and Katie had been invited too, and now they watched with some anxiety as Paul sipped, added another pinch of spice and then sniffed at the steam rising from the pot.

"Can I help?" asked Katie, unable to control herself anymore.

"Nope."

"But I'm sure I could do something..."

"Let him get on with it," said Margaret, smiling. Katie dragged herself away from the stove and sat down next to David, who filled her glass to the brim with red wine.

"Got this in Eskdale last week," he explained and added under his breath, "might help us get supper down."

"I heard that," muttered Paul. Tactful as ever, Margaret decided to change the subject.

"How are you getting along here in Bearsdale?" she asked Tom.

"O.K." he replied, stretching out his long legs under the oak table. "You know, when they sent for me from Canada, to manage the paper mill here, I thought I might hate it. The British were pretty stand offish, they told me. But I was wrong. Everyone here is real kind."

David smiled. "Not everyone. We've got Elijah. He's an old hill farmer lives up towards Holmesdale, hates everyone."

"There's Rowse too, the schoolmaster," put in Katie, "I met him today, he was never exactly forthcoming, but I've never seen him in a worse mood..."

The back door was flung open and there was Rowse. He took no notice whatever of anyone else, but marched straight over to David and waved a large document in his face.

"Have you read this?" he demanded. David glanced at it and handed it back.

"The Nuclear Safety Report," he said calmly. "Yes, I have, as a matter of fact." Visibly trembling with outrage, Rowse glowered down at him, his eyes glittering in his great craggy face like a bird of prey.

"Are you aware what nuclear wastes can do? The mountain eagle for example. It lives largely on fish. Fish live in the stream and the power plant will pour its wastes into it."

"Look, they've been into it, they've made tests, and there's absolutely no danger," David said calmly.

But Rowse had the bit between his teeth now and there was no stopping his flood of fury. "Accidents can happen!" he exclaimed. "A nuclear pile can explode. Oh, they use a less dramatic term for it. They call it critical instability, I believe. Whatever they call it, however, the effects are these. Radio-active wastes are released into the atmosphere."

"I know all this Mr Rowse. I have read this report. The risk of nuclear damage they say is negligible." There was no reply for a moment as Rowse paced up and down the little room like a caged tiger. Then he struck the oaken table such a heavy blow that the plates rattled.

"Negligible!" he exploded.

"Yes, negligible," said David strongly, before Rowse got under way again. "There's one chance in ten million of anything going wrong. If it did, there would be plenty of warning. The temperature in the pile would start to rise. There would be time to flood the whole system."

Glancing round, Rowse snatched up the empty wine bottle and shook it in David's astonished face. "What about the wild life, the deer — the salmon and trout in the streams? I've seen results of abusing nature in Africa. The soil eroding, species after species of wild animal vanishing forever in the face of what they call progress. I thought you were supposed to stop that!"

"I am," said David.

Rowse turned on him. "Then why did you not stop that — that foul thing being built?" he demanded.

"Because, it's perfectly safe, Mr Rowse," said David quietly. Rowse strode to the door. He turned in the doorway, still brandishing the wine bottle.

"As soon as I came here I saw that evil place going up. I protested, but they wouldn't listen. You won't listen now. I have not been able to stop them building it, but I will stop it working, I promise you. Good day!" Then he was gone, slamming the door so hard behind him that the house seemed to shake in its foundations. David turned to Tom with a rueful smile.

"Sorry about that," he said. "Rowse is, well, he's a bit strange."

"I would put it more strongly than that," said Margaret in dismay. "Do you think he means what he says?"

"I'm sure he does," said David lightly, "but I don't know what he thinks he can do."

In fact, Rowse was not long in proving exactly what he could do. The following morning Katie was riding along by the Eskdale road when a lorry drew up behind her and a young man leaned out of the cab.

"Scuse me!" he called cheerfully. "Can you put me on the road to Scoresby Power Plant? I think I've

108

gone out of my way.''

Katie brought Nero round, ''Sure,'' she said.
''Go down into the next village, that's Eskdale, cross
the bridge, first left — it's about six kilometres up the
road.''

''Thanks,'' said the driver, putting the clutch in
to go. ''See you. Don't fall off!'' He drove away, and
Katie put Nero into a canter. In a few moments she
had forgotten all about this encounter, but she was
never to forget what followed.

The driver took his lorry as Katie had directed,
down to the bridge. Here he had to screech to a
sudden halt with a squeal of brakes. Across the
bridge a sturdy barrier of oil drums had been set up,
and behind it stood a small crowd of country people
bearing banners. Their message was *'Justice for
Bearsdale'*, and *'No Pollution'* and *'Atomic Energy*

Out!' In front stood Rowse and Elijah, arms, folded, glaring at the lorry in unison.

"Where are you going?" Rowse demanded with ominous calm.

"Scoresby Power Plant," said the driver in bewilderment.

"I thought so," chimed in Elijah. "Better turn round and go back the way you came."

"Why mate?" asked the driver, glancing from one stony face to another, still more baffled.

"Because I say so," said Rowse. "Also because the people of Bearsdale are not letting any traffic in or out of Scoresby from now on." Elijah grunted in approval.

The driver let out a hoot of laughter. "You must be joking!" But it was clear that he was not.

"I would recommend you to turn round and go back the way you came," Rowse continued. "We are not permitting any work to proceed at Scoresby until we have presented our protest to Parliament."

"Parliament?"

"That is correct. Until we get a reply — a favourable reply, we shall block this road. The only road to Scoresby. So you had best turn round and go back."

****

"So you see," said Sergeant Morris to David the next morning. "We're facing a pretty tricky situation." They were smoking their pipes together in David's kitchen, while Paul made a show of peeling potatoes at the sink and listened to their conversation. "I've only got six men altogether," Sergeant Morris went on, "and that's not enough to

110

see traffic through.''

"Surely you could get more men sent in," said David.

"Of course, we could!" exclaimed Morris, "but our job is to prevent violence, if we can. These people are like the anti-hunting lot, David, there's a good deal in what they have to say. What they're doing may be illegal but if we tackle them head on there will be trouble. The whole anti-pollution thing is an extremely dicey issue at present, and my orders are to play it cool.''

"But they're blocking the road," put in Paul.

"One road, Paul," said Morris, looking up at him. "The only usable road into Scoresby. The trouble is, Rowse has such a hold on this place. You must have noticed how — independent the people are here." David grinned and nodded. "So we must use force only as a last resort," Morris went on. "Which is why I'm talking to you.''

Still grinning to himself, David tapped his pipe bowl gently into the ashtray. "I was wondering when you would come to the point.''

The Sergeant hummed and hawed, obviously having difficulty in choosing his words. "We need a helicopter," he blurted out at last, "and you've got one . . .''

"So have the Forces.''

"No, we've been into that," said Morris, the words coming easily now. "It's too — too Government. If the Press got hold of it — or the media.''
for time. If we can get stuff through to Scoresby, and not have a confrontation with Rowse and his

"Yes I see," said David thoughtfully. "But we can't go flying stores in for ever.''

"Of course not," said Morris. "We're playing for time. If we can get stuff through to Scoresby, and

111

not have a confrontation with Rowse and his people . . ."

"They'll get tired of blocking the road!" Before Morris could add anything further, David was through to Colin on the radio.

"No problem!" Colin breezed through the speaker. "I can take two hundred and fifty kilo each trip, and make five or six trips each day if you want me to. Sure! Just get whatever you want sent to me. I'll see to the rest."

Later that morning, Colin's helicopter lifted swiftly from its landing place and sped off over the peaks towards Scoresby. Rowse watched it go as he stood with his men at the bridge and realised its significance immediately.

"Looks as if it's not workin' don't it?" muttered Elijah, darkly. "Our blockade I mean."

"No!" exploded Rowse. "You told me you would all stand by me! You said you would help me fight."

But Elijah was unmoved. "I got my work to do," he said solidly. "Reckon we all 'ave. You can do whatever you like, Mr. Rowse. I'm off!"

The protesters shuffled amongst themselves, turning to go; hill farmers and shepherds, the village baker, the man who ran the local garage, and the boy who delivered the milk. Rowse stood facing them, the wind ruffling his grey hair, his eyes wild.

"All right, go!" he raved. "I won't stop you! Go back to your homes — I know what to do." They drifted away and Rowse was left alone. "The Lord spoke in his anger," he murmured, "and they were smitten. The unclean thing must be swept away."

Two hours later, Colin was on the phone to David. "Good!" David exclaimed. "Fine — three more trips should look after that first lorry load.

Sure it costs! I'll get Scoresby to foot the bill.'' David rang off, grinning. "Rowse can go on blocking roads as long as he likes," he told Paul. "With Colin flying in all they need at Scoresby, he'll soon get tired of it, I expect."

Paul shook his head. "I'm not so sure. He's a stayer." He wiped the last of the dishes and hung up his cloth.

"Well, it won't do him much good now will it?" remarked David. "Anyway, at the moment there's a job for us to do." Paul looked up enquiringly. "The Fisheries people want us to look at the river. There have been some complaints from anglers."

"Trout not rising?"

"Not flourishing, anyway," said David, pulling on his jacket. "Let's run up there, and have a look."

Meanwhile, Margaret was going through her appointments book at Scarsdale, while Katie, frowning with concentration, struggled with a jersey she was knitting for Paul.

"Barton's got a bit of trouble," observed Margaret. "His cattle have sore mouths and they're off their feed. I think I'll go out there now."

When she arrived at Barton's farm, Margaret examined his herd. "Given up blocking bridges with Rowse have you?" she asked.

"Oh aye," said Barton, lighting up his pipe. "Once the chopper came in on it, there was no future in that." Margaret was peering closely at the cows' mouths. They looked swollen and painful, but all her experience could not give her a clue to the cause.

"How long have they been like this?" she asked Barton.

"They've been off their food for days," he replied. "Mouths look sore, don't they?"

"Yes," said Margaret then, struck by a sudden

113

thought. "Where do they drink?"

"Down there o'course, at the stream."

Further down the valley, David and Paul were wading thigh deep in the Otterburn. First David made a cast, and then Paul, but they had no luck for a while. Suddenly, a trout rose to Paul's line. He reeled in swiftly, then let the line go, as the big trout ran for it.

"Hold him!" cried David. Paul braced himself against the stream and played the trout with remarkable skill. Beaming at David's praise he brought it in. David gaffed it and they carried it over to the rocks which bounded the stream.

"I don't like the look of it," said Paul, after a brief examination. Its mouth and gills were swollen and its belly had an unhealthy colour.

"Now and then you get a dud one," remarked David. "Let's have another go."

They waded back in. An hour later they had caught three trout, and the fish lay side by side on the rocks in front of them.

"Diseased," said David quietly. "All of them. Look at their gills — and their mouths."

"No wonder people have been complaining," said Paul. David looked down the stream and then up at the mountains.

"I'm taking these fish to Margaret," he said at last. "She may be able to help."

"Want me to come along?" asked Paul hedgily.

"Not if you don't want to," David said slightly surprised.

"I'm going to the pictures with Katie tonight," explained Paul. "You can spare me can't you?"

"Course I can," said David, packing the trout into a plastic container. "Be careful with that buggy of yours though. Try tc stay on four wheels."

114

By the time David reached Margaret it was almost five o'clock, but before he could tell her anything Margaret had news for him about Barton's herd.

"I think it's radiation sickness," she said. "It's a bit outside my field, but I would swear . . ."

David broke in urgently. "Look at these trout, would you say they were suffering from radiation?"

She examined them closely, then looked up with troubled eyes. "Yes I would." David pulled a map of the park from his breast pocket.

"I know what you're thinking. Here's Barton's place — this is the stream his cattle drink at. Here's where I've caught the trout. Now go upstream. What do you find?"

"Tom Barry's Mill, Carter's place — and Scoresby Power Station."

"Scoresby Nuclear Power Station," corrected David. Silence fell between them.

"So Rowse was right," said Margaret softly. "It is polluting." At that moment the telephone rang. Margaret answered it; then handed it to David without a word. It was Rowse, speaking from a telephone box.

"I was told you were there, Mr Martin," he said. "Now listen to me very carefully, as I haven't much time. I'm going to plant an explosive device in Scoresby Power Station. No loss of life you understand, just a nuclear spillage. Enough to close down that place for good, and save us all from a nuclear disaster. It's no use trying to stop me, Mr Martin — I've blocked the only road in, and I've cut the place off by phone. By the time you've cleared the road, Mr Martin, the explosion will have taken place. It will be a big one — you'll hear it in Scarsdale, and you'll know that I've won."

The line went dead and David replaced the receiver. After a long pause, Margaret said, "I heard what he was saying, David."

David thought of the radio transmitter in his landrover. "I can stop this," he said decisively. "Colin can help."

But Margaret was blocking his way. "Let him do it, David," she pleaded. David stared down at her in amazement.

"Do you know what you're saying?"

Margaret was trembling, but she was determined to have her say. "Yes I do," she said. "Don't you see? That place is poisoning everything! Those trout you showed me — the cattle up at Bartons. They're diseased, David, and it's Scoresby that's doing it."

"We don't know that."

Margaret almost spat at him. "What else can it be? You know what happened to those Japanese — the fisherman caught in the fall out when they tested the hydrogen bomb. It's happening here, and we ought to stop them."

Now David spoke and with immense force. "Margaret, if we let him he'll let a flood of radio active waste into the valley. The whole place will become a desert, perhaps for years. Do you want that to happen. Do you!" She remained silent, looking at him stubbornly. "I'm going to get in touch with Colin. His helicopter can get us to Scoresby in ten minutes — less. I'll take Sergeant Morris with me. Maybe we can talk Rowse out of it. We've got to try anyway. It's all we can do."

He pushed past her and within moments had got through to Colin and told him to stand by. Then he dashed back to the house to phone Morris and asked him to get to the landing place as soon as he possibly could. As he rang off and made for the door,

Margaret touched his sleeve.

"Be careful, won't you?" she asked.

David smiled. "Of course! I don't want trouble, any more than you do." Then he was gone. Margaret watched him jump into his landrover and make off in a cloud of dust. She turned back to the room and the phone began to ring again.

"Jacksons," she answered automatically, then her expression changed. "Are you sure Tom? Look, don't move — just stay where you are. I'll pick you up — no I can't explain now! Just wait for me — I'll be with you in ten minutes. Bye!" Without more ado, she rushed out of her house, leapt into the Rangerover and made off like greased lightening. What Tom had told her could make all the difference — if only she could get to Rowse in time.

****

Rowse crouched by the security fence, out of sight of the gate, and produced a large pair of wire cutters from his haversack. He cut the wire close to the ground, diving into a rocky gully as the sound of a forklift truck approached and then passed by. Then he was through, carrying the bulky haversack. He crept quietly towards one of the immense buildings of the power plant.

Nobody noticed the big craggy man in his dark tweed suit as he entered the central building by a side exit. Here the great reactor stood, alone and unattended, towering like a steel colossus into the air, with its cooling coils, its numerous gauges and dials, and its massive nuclear casing. Rowse had done his homework and knew exactly what had to be done. He took a set of tools from the haversack, carefully opened a panel and exposed one of the

117

control elements. Then he gingerly removed a bundle of dynamite sticks from the haversack — fifteen kilos of high explosive — and a detonating device. He positioned the charge and started to set the detonator.

Thirty kilometres away, Morris sprinted from his police car to where David was looking at a map

with Colin. All three ran for the helicopter, and strapped themselves in. It took off and flew towards Scoresby. Margaret saw it fly over as she leapt out of her car to meet Tom outside his forest hut.

"No time to explain now," she gasped. "I'll tell you what's happening as we go. Hop in!"

Colin gazed out across the mountain landscape. Range after range extended into a bluish haze, cloud shadowed and magnificent, broken only by the loose stone walls of high pastures and cut by rushing streams.

"How far now?" asked David.

"Not far, five minutes," replied Colin briefly. David exchanged glances with Morris. Every moment counted now. The chopper began to descend. "There it is," Colin said. As they flew in, David spotted a large man slipping out of the reactor building and look up at them.

"Rowse!" he shouted. Colin was bringing the helicopter straight down into the midst of the complex, and Rowse, realising who it was, ran. But as he did so the chopper landed, and David and Morris sprang out after him.

"This way!" yelled Morris. He had seen Rowse dash into the turbine building.

Rowse ran for his life, up steel ladders, past the great humming turbines, across giddy heights, higher and higher into the vast building. He had a good start, but he was not a young man and soon his breath was coming in short heavy gasps, and he had to hold onto the steel railings for support. Still he climbed on, ever upwards, with David and Morris hard at his heels, until he emerged onto the roof.

Trapped on that wide concrete expanse, he turned at bay as David and Morris approached him.

"Don't come any closer!" he gasped. "I've planted a bomb in the core of the reactor and this radio device controls it. If you come a step closer, I'll detonate it at once, releasing a flood of radiation. People will die, Mr. Martin — thousands of them!"

David stayed where he was. "You told me there would be no loss of life," Rowse's face had lost all of its colour. His mad eyes stared at David, almost without recognition.

"I'm afraid I was not telling the truth," he said

at last. "I need loss of life, to drive my point home. Thousands of lives will be lost, yes. But millions of lives will be saved in the future. Isn't it worth it?"

****

Margaret drove her Rangerover at top speed up to the security gate. In a few words she explained her purpose. Sirens began to wail and three vehicles of security men began to converge on the reactor building. Before they reached it, however, Margaret suddenly brought the Rangerover to a halt.

"There they are!" she cried, pointing upwards. Three tiny figures were standing near the edge of the roof of the turbine building. Tom and Margaret dashed into it, with the security men close behind. On the roof, Rowse, David and Morris were frozen still as death. David and Morris dared not make a move, for Rowse's sunken eyes were fixed on them, and his hand was on the trigger of the detonating device.

"Don't move," he said. "When I press this, you will die — swiftly. I will die with you. But it will be a swift death — much swifter than death from radiation. I'm sure you would prefer it that way."

Beads of sweat trickled into Morris' eyes as he spoke now. "Mr. Rowse. This won't do you any good. All right, you release a flood of radiation. You'll kill thousands of people. What will that prove?"

"It will prove what a wicked thing nuclear energy is, Sergeant. This country — this Government needs a good fright. This will give them the fright of their lives. They will have to close Scoresby down. They'll have to close every nuclear power plant in Britain — it's worth anything to do that."

"ROWSE!" David and Morris started at the sudden cry and then Margaret and Tom appeared over the top of the steel ladder. Rowse turned his haggard face to meet them.

"Don't move," he whispered. "I can . . ."

"I know what you want to do, " said Margaret brusquely. "Tom has something to say to you. Tom — tell him!"

Tom's face was red and troubled. "It's all my fault, I got reports on pollution weeks ago — before you did, I think. I looked into it, and I didn't like what I saw one little bit. So I did a bit of research, and I traced the trouble." He paused to gather breath. "It's Mercury Perchlorate, one of the chemicals we use at the mill. We won't be using it any more — in fact, I've closed the place down this afternoon until we can put in some new gear."

Now, David spoke. "It's all right, Rowse," he said gently. "It's not this Power Station. It's the paper mill, and that's being put right now. This place is doing no harm."

Minutes seemed to tick by as Rowse stared at David. Then his gaze fell on Morris and Tom and Margaret and finally the security men. They stood there looking back at him, waiting for his decision. Then with a swift gesture he crushed the delicate mechanism in his powerful hand and burst into tears.

****

The weekend came up on them, as hot and dusty as ever. David and Margaret had driven up into the mountains behind Scarsdale for the day. Now they sat in a heathery coombe with Paul and Katie, idly gazing out across the green and grey landscape that stretched beneath them. Margaret had laid on a cold fowl and French bread and butter, and some cheese, and David was opening a bottle of wine.

"Looks as if we missed something yesterday"

said Paul, splitting open a hunk of bread and spreading it liberally with butter. Turning onto his side, he asked David what had happened to Rowse.

"He'll be all right, I hope. They've taken him into hospital for a check-up. But I don't think they'll lock him up. He's been under great strain for some time. He's very ill."

"Is he so mad?" said Margaret at last. "Isn't there a lot in what he had to say?"

David smiled wryly. "Of course, there is, that's the trouble. There's no easy answer to this sort of thing, we've got to have energy or we'd all freeze and starve, and coal and oil won't last for ever."

"So we've got to have Nuclear Power?"

"Exactly," said David, finally managing to remove the cork from the bottle with a resounding pop. "But Rowse is right in a way. It is dangerous, and we do risk wrecking the environment." He grinned suddenly. "I'm getting too serious for such a lovely day. Here, have some of this. "They drink wine in Mediterranean countries because the water's unsafe. Do you think it will come to that here one day?"

"Might not be so bad!" put in Paul. He lifted his glass for filling.

Katie was not drinking. She was gazing upwards, shading her eyes against the sun.

"Look," she whispered. High up, against the summer clouds, wheeled the mountain eagle that Rowse had pointed out to her.

"I hope they'll always be with us, don't you?" said David. They watched together as the eagle spread his great wings and rode the wind, higher and higher above Bearsdale. He was safe from pollution— at least for the time being. David meant to keep it that way.

122

CHAPTER SIX

FIRE!

It was late September now, and still it had not rained. The pastures were dry and parched, the forests like tinder. Even the streams had shrunk to mere trickles with pools of stagnant water lying stranded among the rocks. David, driving his landrover across the moor track by Rodale Forest, was reminded of one enormous powder barrel — the least spark would turn it into a raging inferno. He saw a neat row of tents pitched close to the edge of the woods under the shade of the trees, and drove over to investigate.

A young man in T-shirt and jeans was playing football with a crowd of small boys, a big retriever rushing around them with his tail flailing wildly. One boy was busy tending a camp fire over which hung a huge iron kettle.

"Hello!" said David, approaching the young man. "I'm David Martin, Park Ranger. May I have a word?"

"Of course," said the young man. He tossed the ball to one of the boys and extended his hand. "I'm Peter Bultitude, Reverend Peter Bultitude as a matter of fact. St Swithuns, Coventry."

"How do you do," said David. "Adventure group are they?"

"No," Peter replied. "They're my choristers as

a matter of fact. How can I help you?"

"How long are you planning to stay here?"

"We arrived the day before yesterday for a long weekend. Got to shoot off this afternoon, I'm afraid."

"Well, watch that fire, won't you?" asked David. "The whole place is so dry with this drought."

"Of course I will — I know the Country Code." He beamed in a jolly manner and then as David was going called, "I say, you don't happen to know the test result do you? We're so out of touch here!"

David laughed. "We won — by exactly one wicket," he said, climbing into the landrover. He drove off and Peter began to round up his charges.

"Come on now, pack it in! We've got a long hike this morning, and then a very long journey home. No point in wearing ourselves out in the sun!"

David drove on, bent on a more disagreeable task. He had coaxed the County Council into agreeing to his plans for the Bridle Way. They had even agreed to his name for it — Bearsdale Way, and given him a modest grant against the cost of setting it all up. Of the sixteen hill farmers David had seen, no less than fifteen had agreed to let the way run across their land — admittedly after much persuasion. Only one had remained obdurate. Elijah had stood firm in the face of anything David could say, and if Elijah went on saying no, the whole plan would fall down, for there was no way round for the bridle path other than right through the middle of Elijah's hill pastures.

Hoping, halfheartedly, to wear him down with persistence, David had decided to have yet another try. He turned up the stone lane that led to Elijah's farm. Timber lay asleep in the yard as David arrived, but woke as soon as David got out of the landrover. His hackles rose and he growled in a menacing way. Elijah was tinkering underneath an ancient tractor.

"I know why yer 'ere," he growled. "The answer's still no. So you may as well save yer breath." This was an unpromising start, but David was determined not to be put off.

"It seems a pity," he said, lighting his pipe. "People need a bridle path, and if they don't get it, they'll do ten times as much damage as they do at present, leaving gates open, spoiling the hay."

"Aye well, there's an answer to that i'nt there?" said Elijah, crossly. He paused in his work to peer up from beneath the tractor. "They needn't come. Then there wouldn't be any trouble."

"People must have holidays."

"No they don't!" Elijah cut in rudely. "I never wanted one. What do they want to come down 'ere 'or, with their cars and their charabangs, turnin' whole place upside down? My grandpa never stirred out of Bearsdale all 'is life, 'cept to go fight in t'war, and nor did my father."

"That's different," said David patiently. "Most people have to live in towns. They have to work in shops and offices and factories."

Elijah was unpersuaded. "Well let them stay there," he muttered, getting back to his work. "If they wants 'olidays, let them go somewhere else. I'm not 'avin them on my land."

David saw that it was hopeless and climbed back into his landrover.

"And next time, don't smoke in my yard!" came Elijah's parting cry. "I don't want my 'ay set on fire!" David grimaced and drove out of the yard, with his ears burning. He was seen safely off the

125

premises by Timber who stood at the gateway barking furiously. "Danged Wardens!" grumbled Elijah, getting on with the oily workings of his tractor. "Wasn't no such things when I was a lad!"

David reached Grimsdyke in poor spirits to find Paul painstakingly knotting his tie in the kitchen mirror. He was wearing a smart sports jacket and trousers and a clean shirt. David had never seen him make such an effort since his arrival in Bearsdale.

"Is all this quite necessary?" he asked, laughing. "She's not exactly royalty, after all."

"I know," Paul retorted, "but she is my Aunt! I haven't seen her for nearly three months, and she has come all the way from London for the weekend to see me, and I've not written much. So the least I can do is make some sort of effort."

Three months ago. Was it only three months? Looking at Paul, David felt disturbed by the thought of Aunt Carol's arrival. Paul had grown in those three months — physically and mentally too. Fresh air and exercise had filled him out and given him a healthy tan and a shock of extra freckles. Responsibility and hard work had given him steadiness and a mature approach to problems. In fact, Paul was just the sort of son David would have liked to have had, if he had ever married. Still, it was no use thinking of that now.

"Take it easy in that beach buggy," said David. "You may be used to it, but I'm sure your Aunt Carol isn't."

"I will," Paul replied. He hurried to the door and then stopped. "I'll take her straight to the Jacksons. You're coming to lunch there aren't you?"

"Wouldn't miss it for the world," said David gravely and added as an afterthought. "Don't get rough with her will you?"

"Rough?" said Paul, scandalised. "Of course not! Who do you think I am?"

"I know she wants you to give up all this, and go back with her to London."

Paul stuck out his chin stubbornly. "It's my life. I'm going to stand my ground."

David watched him from the window as he climbed into the beach buggy and drove off towards the station. This was the moment of truth all right. Paul's aunt, he knew, wanted him to give up Bearsdale and go back with her to London. With a sigh, he picked up the phone.

"Are you suggesting that I should take sides?" Margaret demanded. David's call had come through just as she was putting an apple pie in the oven, and she was not in the mood for lending a sympathetic ear.

"I just thought you should be in the picture," said David. "You know that Paul was brought up by this aunt of his. Well, she wants him to go into the family business. That's why she's coming in fact."

"To talk him into going back to London with her?"

"That's right," said David glumly.

"But he's eighteen!" exploded Margaret. "He's got a mind of his own. Besides, this place is his life, David. Oh, I know he was all over the place at first. But he's settled into it wonderfully — don't you think so, too?"

"Yes, I do," said David thoughtfully, "but it's his life. He must do whatever he thinks is best."

By now Paul had picked his aunt up at the ramshackle halt that passed for a railway station in Bearsdale, and they were bowling along the road above the Eskdale valley. Carol drank in the lush green heathery slopes, and the gaunt mountain ranges marching into the distance.

"Oh do stop!" she cried. She was an extremely attractive women of thirty-nine. Her scarlet open necked shirt and beautifully cut suede suit proclaimed her for what she was — a highly successful young business woman and photographer. Carol specialised in stately homes and jetset holidays. She had taken shots of English country houses and Scottish castles and French chateaux as well as Italian palaces and Mediterranean islands. But Bearsdale was altogether something of a surprise to her.

"Stop!" she cried again. "oh, this is simply magnificent! I must take some pictures." She unslung a fine Japanese camera and began shooting, working at great speed. "I can see why you love it so much here. I just don't know how you will be able to bear leaving it." Paul glanced at her sharply, and frowned, but she seemed unaware of what she had said.

"Let's move on," she murmured. "I'm dying to meet your boss — David Martin, isn't he?"

"That's right. He's coming to lunch with us."

"Good! Then I'll meet him. What are the Jacksons like?"

"You'll see," said Paul. "They'll make you very comfortable anyway. Home cooking — I often drop round."

Margaret was setting out the table and Katie giving the glasses a final polish when Paul arrived with Carol.

"Anyone cure a giraffe of a sore throat!" he called out as he burst through the door.

"That could only be Paul," Margaret remarked to Katie. She turned to greet him just as Carol came in. "Hello, I'm Margaret Jackson, and this is my

128

daughter, Katie."

"Hello, Katie," said Carol warmly, shaking hands with her.

"Hello, Mrs. Graham," Katie replied coolly. She knew why Aunt Carol had come.

"Oh, call me Carol, for goodness sake!" laughed Carol. There was a momentary silence.

"I'll show you your room," said Margaret, picking up Carol's pigskin cases and going upstairs.

"Honestly, I've never seen such a delightful house," cooed Carol, "Seventeenth century, isn't it?"

"Most of it, yes," said Margaret leading the way. "Some of it's even older." Then they were gone. Katie flung herself onto the sofa.

"So that's the dragon!" she laughed. Paul frowned at her. "Come to breathe fire on you — whisk you away."

"She may try," muttered Paul, leaning moodily against the table. "But she won't succeed."

"Are you so sure of that?"

Paul nodded slowly. "Quite sure. When she sees this is my scene, she won't push it."

"She has come all the way from London," said Katie. Paul looked at her in amazement.

"You don't want me to go do you?"

"Of course not," she replied, smiling at him. "I hope you'll always stay here. But you must do what you think best. Of course, if you prefer London."

"I don't!" Paul jumped up and strode over to the window. "You know I love it here."

Katie could see that he was disturbed and thoughtful. "Well, I should let Aunt Carol say whatever she has to," she advised, "and then play it by ear."

At the camp, the boys were packing up. Peter was piling them and their gear into his truck.

"Come on!" he bellowed. "Put that fire out, and get those tents folded. Robert, stop mucking about and get Max into the truck."

"Aw, just one more run!" cried Robert. "He's got a long journey in front of him. Please sir!"

Peter sighed, exasperated. "Alright. Just a quick one, mind you. Bill get that tent packed or I'll have the hide off you."

Two boys were stamping the fire out and Robert seized a stick from the edge of it. One end of the stick

was glowing very faintly, as he threw it for Max. It went further than Robert had intended, into the undergrowth that grew thickly at the edge of the wood. Max bounded after it, but he was not very bright and could not find it. He rushed up and down excitedly in the heather, stopping to sniff now and then at a tree trunk. Then he heard Robert whistle to him and gave up.

Peter climbed into the cab and Robert hoisted Max into the back; then the truck, full of shouting, cheering boys, bumped off over the field to the road.

Nestled in the heather, the stick lay glowing, a thin wisp of smoke curling from its orange-red tip . . .

It was at about this time that David arrived at Scarsdale for lunch. He sat, a little stiffly, facing Carol, while Paul and Katie tucked silently into Margaret's roast beef.

"Of course, Dr Johnson was right," Carol was saying. "The man who is tired of London is tired of life. The woman too!" she added as an afterthought, laughing at her little joke.

Katie remained dour-faced. "I would hate to live in London. Millions of houses. No air."

"You're so wrong, my dear," said Carol, pleasantly. "There's the river — perfectly delightful in the summer — and the parks."

"I still think I would hate it," said Katie as politely as possible.

"Well, of course. I can imagine how much you love it here," laughed Carol, sipping at her wine. "I'm sure Paul will miss it terribly when I take him back to the big city." There was an awkward silence. David decided to change the subject.

"I hear you've been taking lots of pictures for your magazine."

"My dear, I don't own one!" exclaimed Carol. "I work freelance, you know. Of course, John — that's my husband — runs a publishing firm. Lovely offices in Hampstead. Not a stone's throw away

131

from where we live. You'd like it there, Paul."

Stone-faced, Paul addressed himself silently to his beef.

"Did Paul show you Eskdale on your way here?" enquired Margaret hastily.

"Oh yes," said Carol, enthusiastically. "I've never seen more beautiful country. I'm going to take masses of pictures back to London with me."

Katie glared at her. "Great! They'll remind you of where Paul is working." She went back to her plate, toying with her food.

Carol was no fool. She could see that Paul was acutely embarrassed by Katie's hostility, and decided on a direct retort.

"They could be a splendid reminder of good times for Paul, too," she said, looking pleasantly but very pointedly at Paul. David could bear it no longer.

"I'll take you out this afternoon if you like," he said, "to Kite's Brow. Wonderful view from up there."

"Great," said Carol. "I would really like that."

Hidden by the heather and trees of Rodale Woods, small tongues of flame were at that very moment beginning to flicker around the forgotten stick. A plume of smoke lifted in the light breeze, but in this remote spot far from the main mountain passes there was no-one to see it and give warning. A tangle of briars crackled and caught fire, burning briefly but furiously. Trickles of fire began to run through the parched heather to lick at the foot of a tall pine . . .

At Scarsdale they had finished lunch and were drinking coffee. "I can see why you love it here," said Carol, "and I can imagine what it's like working for David — it must be fun."

David smiled. "He's doing extremely well here. Though rash of me to say so, I suppose."

"Yes, I'm proud of you, Paul," said Carol. "But what of the future? Do you really want to make this your career?"

Paul studied the tablecloth and shrugged. "I don't know," he said at last. "Not for sure."

"You know that John has been expanding the business," said Carol, brightly. "He has several branches now. Bristol, Edinburgh, Oxford. Now there's going to be one in New York."

This piece of news made Paul start up with interest. "I didn't know that!"

Carol smiled. "It was only decided last week. Derek Crawford is going to run it. You met him at our house once I think." Paul nodded. "He's going to need an assistant and your uncle thinks it would be nice to have a Graham out there."

"You mean, me?" exclaimed Paul.

She laughed. "Why not? You'd learn as you went along. Derek would show you the ropes. Couldn't you work with him?" Paul nodded again, he did not know what to say.

"I don't want to lose you Paul," said David. "But I must say, it sounds a wonderful chance."

"Yes it does," Paul agreed thoughtfully. He could sense Katie's eyes boring into him, but he did not look at her.

In Rodale Woods, a pine tree flared up, its cones and branches burning furiously. The fire fed greedily on the dry debris underneath, flashed up through the parched branches of neighbouring pines and spread rapidly to their crowns. Soon, nearly thirty pines were burning together, throwing streams of fire high into the air. Glowing branches crashed to the shimmering ground — spreading further destruction. The birds flew afraid from the raging furnace, and startled squirrels and deer ran frantically for safety, but no human being was near at hand.

****

Back in the office at Grimsdyke, Paul was trying to make up his mind about his future. He tapped out a few lines on the typewriter, then moved restlessly to the window. Outside the beautiful mountain landscape lay gleaming in the bright sunlight. It was home to him now, and more than that, the only truly rewarding work he had ever known. Bearsdale had become part of him — the mountains, the hill farms, and the steady dependable people — even Elijah. There was David too, whom he liked and respected so much, and Margaret, so quiet and friendly, and Katie.

On the other hand, he had not seen much of the world and the thought of New York excited him. What would it be like, working for a publishing firm in that famous city? What would New York be like?

"Made up your mind?" Katie was standing in the doorway, in breeches and boots, ready for riding. The wind was ruffling her hair. He had never seen her look so attractive. "Well?" she repeated. "Have you decided?"

"No," said Paul, confused. "I'm trying to make up my mind. Not very successfully I'm afraid." He turned to look out of the window again, avoiding Katie's gaze.

"I wouldn't go," she said abruptly.

"Easy for you to say that! I'm the one who has to go, or not."

"Look, you'll be doing the same work you turned down in London," said Katie. He mumbled an agreement. "Then you twit, what's the difference? In an office in London all day, in an office in New York all day. Think about it!'' Without another word she turned tail and was gone. Paul, his mind in a whirl, tried to get back to his typing.

Meanwhile, David was driving Carol to Kites Brow. The mountains were looking superb in the golden afternoon. ''Fantastic!'' she cried. ''This will keep me going for hours.''

''I'll pick you up whenever you like.''

''No!'' retorted Carol, laughing. ''I'll walk back, if you don't mind. The exercise will do me good.'' He smiled at her and drove off, while she began to take pictures.

Uneasy at heart, David drove homewards. Suddenly, he stopped and jumped out of the land-rover. A hazy smudge of smoke was building up over the mountain peaks to the north. David lifted his binoculars and took a closer look. Pines, burning furiously. He got out his walkie talkie and contacted Paul.

Paul was still typing halfheartedly when David's call came through, clear and urgent.

''Fire in Rodale Woods, under Eskdale! Call Colin, tell him to have a look and get here as soon as you can!''

Deep in the forest, the fallow deer were grazing under the watchful gaze of the biggest stag of the herd. Hunting was not allowed in Bearsdale, though from time to time the deer had to be culled. Even so, the deer were not accustomed to people and were extremely shy. Though their deadliest enemy, the wolf, had been wiped out centuries ago in Britain, they were always on the alert for danger. Now, the big stag paused suddenly in his grazing and lifted his great antlered head. He turned his nose into the

135

wind, his nostrils flaring.

Something was in the air. This stag was no veteran; he was scarcely three years old and for the moment he could not understand the message in the wind. The herd was looking towards him for guidance. He took a few uncertain steps, sniffing the breeze. Then he tossed his head, baffled. It was the smell of fire. He had never experienced fire before, but generations of instinct welled up within him as he turned again, frightened now, into the wind. This time it brought with it a gust of smoke and a faint but infinitely ominous sound. The great stag fled, terrified through the woods, and the herd stampeded after him, crashing through the undergrowth, making blindly for safety, they knew not where.

David drove his landrover at top speed towards the fire. He stopped appalled at the size of it, and got onto the walkie talkie again.

"Paul!" he called. "This is a big one! Round up the forest people, get Margaret's help if you can — and Tom's lot at the mill. We're going to need all the help we can get!"

Looking back to the fire, he suddenly noticed a rider galloping down the mountain track. Katie had decided on a good canter with Nero to settle her mind, but as she had taken him along the ridge above Rodale, she had seen the forest alight. Now she was riding like the wind towards the landrover as it ascended the steep track. David leaned out as she rode up.

"Katie!" he cried. "Get hold of everyone you can find and send them here! Hurry!" She nodded and galloped past him and David hurried on towards the forest.

136

Unaware of the unfolding drama, Carol lay back on a rock, breathing deeply. She had climbed up the southern slope of Bell's Crag to get a better view and now, worn out by her unusual exertion she slipped into a drowsy sleep. The crag had hidden even the faintest puff of smoke from her.

Cursing to himself, David drove to within metres of the fire and leapt out. Well over a hectare of forest had been engulfed. The heat was so tremendous that he could see the very bark blistering and the resin bubbling on trees well clear of the perimeter of the fire. There was a steady roar as oxygen rushed in to the vast furnace to be consumed and a column of fiery gases rose hundreds of metres into the air.

David caught up a branch and started to feverishly fight the fire, though one man could make no impression whatsoever on that raging holocaust. He didn't stop to think — his job, among other things, was to fight forest fires, and fight it he did — with burning branches falling about him, and trees exploding like bombs from the heart, and sparks showering him . . .

****

Paul took the buggy as fast as it would go through Eskdale forest, bouncing against fallen logs, and charging along tracks that were usually troughs of deep mud, but were now dusty and rutted, as dry as a bone. He sighted a gang of men cutting logs. One almost rolled into him and they shouted at him angrily to mind what he was doing and keep out of the way. The next minute, Paul had told them what was happening. They downed tools, piled into a landrover and shot off without another word. Fire is the enemy of all foresters.

Katie came clear of the forest and rode towards three hill farmers who were gossiping by a gate.

"Fire!" she cried. They turned their sunburned faces to her.

"Where's the fire then!" said one of them calmly. It was Elijah.

"Rodale woods!" she yelled. "It's a big one. David needs all the help he can get!"

"Does 'e now?" said Elijah, squinting up at her. "Then I reckon we 'ad better bury old scores and get on with it." He and his mates piled into an ancient Ford and with a terrible crunching of gears and grinding of metal, the old jalopy hurtled off.

David thought that his back was going to crack. His arms ached badly, his face was blistered and he was almost blinded with sweat. Though almost twenty men and women were now fighting the blaze, they seemed barely able to check it, let alone get it under control. As fast as they succeeded in stamping the edge of it out in one place, it flared up in another, changing the gorse into flaming torches, roaring up the dry pines and turning their tops into a raging inferno. Then Elijah turned up in his ancient Ford. Behind him came a procession of equally battered vehicles full of hill farmers, he had rounded up on the way.

"Thought you might do wi' a bit of 'elp," he said gruffly. David grinned at him through the filth and sweat and they fought the fire side by side.

Katie rode back towards Rodale Forest and into its outskirts, a small wood called Scurry Copse. This was the quickest short cut she knew to Eskdale village where she hoped to round up more helpers. Suddenly a herd of deer dashed across her path. Led by a big stag, they were charging instinctively towards the

138

nearest stream. But the fire was spreading over the floor of the forest with dreadful speed. Katie saw the stag veer sideways, terrified as the fire advanced to the edge of the clearing. She saw it plunge into a stream, only to find nothing but a mere chain of rocky pools. There was only one way left out of the clearing for the deer, the way she had come in. The deer were too frightened to take it, unless they were made to.

She turned Nero at full gallop to head them into the right direction. The great stag saw her coming and tried to dash past, but riding as she had never done before, Katie managed to get ahead of him and turned him back. The stag dashed for the gap and his herd went after him. In a few moments they were through to safety, but Katie had left it terribly late. The air was now filled with flying ashes, drifting as thick as snow. Nero plunged violently, snorting with terror, and Katie calmed him with a slap on the neck and got him under control. She set him towards the gap, and he responded to her heels, when suddenly a tall pine to her left exploded with a roar of flames.

She came to gradually to find that the top of a fallen pine had pinned her to the ground. Its branches had broken the fall, or she would certainly have been killed. As it was, she was badly cut and her left leg hurt abominably. Nero was nowhere to be seen. She tried to shift the weight across her, but it was hopeless — the log was far too heavy.

There were flames in the clearing now, licking the other side of the stream, and the air was getting hard to breathe. Katie tried with all her might to get clear, her clothes were torn and bloody, ashes were drifting down on her head. Tears sprang to her eyes and she began to cry out in fear.

Paul was almost afraid that his beach buggy would catch fire, as he drove furiously along the forest track to join the fire fighters. The wind was like the breath from a furnace and Paul looked upwards anxiously to see if the fire was crowning — that event most dreaded by all foresters, when the fire catches the tops of the trees and spreads with awe-inspiring rapidity. He saw no sign of it yet, but what he did see was Colin's helicopter. He stopped the buggy and raised his walkie talkie to contact him.

"What can you see?" he asked.

"About three hundred hectares on fire," replied Colin, looking down at the blazing trees below him. "I'm calling in all the help I can find." The helicopter turned and made off, and Paul made to start up the buggy. Even as he did so, he heard a faint cry. He recognised it at once — it was Katie and it was coming from the burning woods of Scurry Copse. Without a thought, except for her safety he abandoned the buggy by the track and plunged into the woods, looking for her.

The bark on the trees about him was catching fire and the air was raining with flying ash. He tore his jacket off as he ran and held it in front of his face. Then he saw Katie lying in a clearing under a log. Her face was bruised and bleeding, but she smiled wanly when she saw him.

"Trust you to turn up," she whispered. "Bad pennies always do, don't they?" Paul fell to his knees and tried to prize the log off her, but it was far too massive to shift. He gazed about the clearing in despair.

Luck was with him, however. Margaret, who had fetched in three car loads of fire fighters, was dashing back for more when she suddenly came across the beach buggy abandoned by the track. She

140

leapt out of her own vehicle and ran over to it. Paul's denim cap was lying on the seat. As she picked it up, looking about her in bewilderment, she heard Paul crying for help. She dropped the cap and sprinted into the forest, dodging burning brands and gasping painfully for breath. Then she saw Katie lying under the log and Paul still trying to lift it off her by brute force. She rushed to help him but it was useless — the enormous log would not budge at all. The main fire was very close now; flames were gushing through the gorse and flashing up the pine trees. With a terrible roar the tops caught fire.

Then inspiration came to Paul. He pulled the walkie talkie from his jacket pocket.

"Colin!" he gasped. "Come in Colin! I'm in a

141

clearing in Scurry Copse — we're in trouble!''

The helicopter circled and flew in low above the Copse with Paul guiding him in on the walkie talkie. Colin saw the small figure of Paul waving at him and he came in closer still.

"Colin!" called Paul. "Use the hoist! Katie's trapped under a log — can you see it?"

"Yes" said Colin, "I can. I'll have a go — standby!" He dropped in the hoist and Paul shackled it swiftly to the log. Then the helicopter went into full throttle and the log began to rise off Katie, slowly at first then more rapidly; and Paul and Margaret dragged her out.

As they bore her away, the forest crowned. Gusts of flame advanced with nightmare speed, flooding the clearing behind them. They rushed Katie to the buggy, got her into it and drove off. Margaret's Rangerover vanished from sight. Then it erupted in an explosion that blew burning fragments in all directions. The whole of Scurry Copse was engulfed in the blaze.

****

"You know what this is," said Margaret. "Punishment for being rude to Paul's Aunt Carol!"

"I wasn't rude!" Katie exclaimed hotly. She was lying on the sofa at Scarsdale, with Margaret sitting close by her, and Paul expertly bandaging her injured leg.

"Well, we won't argue about it," said Margaret, equably. "You're doing a good job there, Paul. Mind you I don't think First Aid is going to be much use to you from now on though, is it? Unless somebody trips up walking down Broadway."

Paul exchanged glances with Katie.

142

"When you gotta go, ow! You gotta go!" said Katie, grinning painfully. "That's all there is to it!" It was at that moment Carol came bursting in, fresh as a daisy, and carrying her camera.

"Well, I spent most of my time sleeping, but I've taken some super shots..." she stopped abruptly as the sight that faced her sunk in. Paul, Katie and Margaret were scarcely recognisable, their faces smudged, their clothes torn and filthy, their hair full of ash.

"Well!" she said, faintly. "It looks as if I've missed something!"

In the forest, David and his companions had at last got the fire under control though it was still burning in on itself. They had made a fire break and the raging flames, deprived of fuel had turned back to consume each other. The foresters and hill farmers had then driven a wedge through the inferno, breaking it into two, and were breaking up the two fragments to take each piece in turn. The fire brigade were busily dowsing the site with hoses but the terrible urgency had gone.

David wiped his dirty face with the grubby shirt he had torn off hours ago. He climbed wearily into his landrover and set out for Scarsdale Farm.

On his arrival, Carol was sitting with Paul and Katie drinking coffee.

"So that's what happened," she was saying, and then she added quietly. "Paul do you think it would be as exciting as this in New York?"

Paul eyed her warily, "I don't know. After all, I've never been."

Carol looked long and hard at Paul, then she smiled quickly and said. "I'm glad I came when I did. And I'm glad you're staying."

At the sight of David, Margaret and Katie

staring at her almost open-mouthed in astonishment, she burst out laughing. "I'm not such an ogre you know! Just let me come up here again some time to take some pictures — that's all I ask!" She kissed Paul warmly and received in return a smudged face.

****

So Paul began his life as a Park Warden. What a crowded three months it had been he reflected. Rabid dogs, convicts, helicopter rescues, near nuclear disasters — they all passed through his mind. He looked at David as he put the kettle on for a coffee, his capable hands and his tanned, broad face — blistered by fire. David had become a solid dependable father to him — no, not a father, he decided — an older brother. He wondered what adventures they would share in the coming months.

He looked at Margaret, searching out a mug for David. Her boots and jeans and blue jersey were smudged and filthy, and her fair hair whitened still further with ashes, but she was laughing merrily. And Katie — Katie was lying on the sofa, her shirt ripped, her face scratched and swollen but her eyes were shining. What did the future hold there, he wondered. He hardly knew, but he knew one thing — he cared very much.

Far away, in the shelter of a quiet glade that the fire had not touched, the stag and his does were grazing. The woods they had been in a few hours before were now a blackened desert. It would be months before fresh grass grew there again, and years before the deep woodlands returned. But nature would heal them in the end, and the deer would graze there again, one day.

Now, rather too late, it began to rain.